D1085574

Bombay Wali

and Other Stories

first fictions series 5

 Canada Council for the Arts **Conseil des Arts du Canada**

 ONTARIO ARTS COUNCIL
CONSEIL DES ARTS DE L'ONTARIO
50 YEARS OF ONTARIO GOVERNMENT SUPPORT OF THE ARTS
50 ANS DE SOUTIEN DU GOUVERNEMENT DE L'ONTARIO AUX ARTS

Guernica Editions Inc. acknowledges the support of
the Canada Council for the Arts and the Ontario Arts Council.
The Ontario Arts Council is an agency of the Government of Ontario. We
acknowledge the financial support of the Government of Canada through
the Canada Book Fund (CBF) for our publishing activities.

Bombay Wali

and Other Stories

VEENA GOKHALE

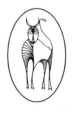

GUERNICA

TORONTO – BUFFALO – BERKELEY – LANCASTER (U.K.) 2013

Copyright © 2013, Veena Gokhale and Guernica Editions Inc.

All rights reserved. The use of any part of this publication, reproduced, transmitted in any form or by any means, electronic, mechanical, photocopying, recording or otherwise stored in a retrieval system, without the prior consent of the publisher is an infringement of the copyright law.

Michael Mirolla, general editor
Guernica Editions Inc.
P.O. Box 117, Station P, Toronto (ON), Canada M5S 2S6
2250 Military Road, Tonawanda, N.Y. 14150-6000 U.S.A.

Distributors:
University of Toronto Press Distribution,
5201 Dufferin Street, Toronto (ON), Canada M3H 5T8
Gazelle Book Services, White Cross Mills,
High Town, Lancaster LA1 4XS U.K.
Small Press Distribution, 1341 Seventh St.,
Berkeley, CA 94710-1409 U.S.A.

First edition.
Printed in Canada.
Legal Deposit – First Quarter

Library of Congress Catalog Card Number: 2012951261

Library and Archives Canada Cataloguing in Publication

Gokhale, Veena
Bombay wali & other stories / Veena Gokhale.

(First fiction series ; 5)
Issued also in electronic format.
ISBN 978-1-55071-672-6

I. Title. II. Series: First fictions series (Toronto, Ont.) ; 5

PS8613.O42B66 2013   C813'.6   C2012-906954-X

To my grandmother, Laxmi Shripad Gokhale,
for telling me fabulous stories
from the Hindu epics under starry skies.

Contents

Bombay Wali   9

Middle Age Jazz and Blues   32

The Tea Drinker   48

Zindagi Itefaq Hai (Life is Chance)   64

Freire Stopped in Bombay   81

Absolution   106

Smoke and Mirrors   121

Snapshot   135

Reveries of a Riot   148

Kathmandu   166

The Room   184

Munni   203

AUTHOR NOTES   210

GLOSSARY   211

ACKNOWLEDGEMENTS   214

PREVIOUSLY PUBLISHED   215

ABOUT THE BOOK   216

ABOUT THE AUTHOR   217

Aai dil hai mushkil jeena yahan,
jara hatke, jara bachke, yeh hai Bombay meri jaan.
Oh my heart, it is difficult to live here;
step aside, be careful, this is Bombay, my beloved.

– Hindi lyrics of an old Bollywood song

Bombay Wali

Gulnar Vaid, Tanya Trivedi and Renuka Rao met at The Wayside Inn for lunch. The three young women were freelance journalists eking out a meagre but interesting living in Bombay.

Renuka pursed her thin lips as she read the menu, which was mostly non-vegetarian and bland. Having grown up on *idli-dosa-rasam* in Madras, she would have preferred eating at the Udipi restaurant down the road. She missed home food now that she lived with a Goan-Christian family in a cramped Paying Guest accommodation in Mahim. But Tanya had insisted that they meet here. Udipi restaurants lacked ambience, she had said. And ambience was more important than mere nourishment.

Renuka cast a half irate, half indulgent glance at Tanya who was studying the menu through her over-sized sunglasses. She took them off only after the sun had gone to bed. A large straw hat worn to protect her pale skin sat at a slight angle on her head. It had drawn attention when they had walked in. Tanya had cut confidently through the stares, going straight to their usual corner table with a street view. It was Renuka who had felt awkward, though no one had paid her much attention.

Gulnar was not looking at the menu at all. Puffing away on a cigarette, she surveyed the motley crowd.

She already knew what she was going to order; she always ate the same thing here — chicken club sandwich with a glass of *limbu-pani*, dubbed fresh lime-water in the menu.

Tanya opened her large purse and looked inside.

"Eight rupees," she announced. "That's what I can spend."

"That's good," ventured Renuka.

"That's fantastic," said Gulnar. "I have 50 rupees for the week and 20 will go on cigs."

"I could lend you money," said Tanya at once.

"You know, I'm going to rob a bank one of these days," said Gulnar. She sat back in her chair and blew a perfect smoke ring.

She should have been an actress, thought Renuka. She wasn't good looking in the conventional sense, but she had a strong presence. And she was outrageous, smoking openly in public.

"Let me be your banker," said Tanya, smiling.

Renuka looked at the menu again. Fortunately the vegetarian items were also the cheapest. She decided on vegetable cutlets, spelt "cutless". They need an editor, she thought, not for the first time.

Renuka and Gulnar lived away from their hometowns and were mostly broke, though they approached their circumstances differently. Gulnar celebrated her situation, wearing never-washed jeans and long, *khadi kurtas* with holes in them, occasionally making a meal out of a packet of peanuts and a banana, while splurging on cigarettes and books. Though a journalist like Renuka and Tanya, her main focus was a novel entitled *Bombay Wali*. Believing that thorough research must precede writing, she spent her days taking in the scene and her evenings writing down her observations.

Fortunately, her boyfriend, Geet, supported this notion. He drove her around the city in his old, but serviceable Fiat, and held her hand through all the diversions — a cabaret in a sleazy Juhu hotel, a séance in a Girgaon *chawl* (tenement) and an all-night *shayari* session held at a rented hall in Khar. They also frequented a wide range of city restaurants. Gulnar had decided that her heroine's parents would own one. But would she be Goan or Gujarati? Muslim or Parsi? Tamilian, Malayali, or for that matter, Chinese? Gulnar could not decide. In any case, Geet's five-figure, accountant's salary aided her explorations.

"Art is more important than life," Gulnar would say from time to time, the pronouncement duly accompanied by a smoke ring. Renuka did not agree. Life made so many demands, where was the room for art? She hated her impoverished existence, the sensation of being afloat rather than grounded. What kept her going was the certain knowledge that things were going to be different in the future. She had a game plan. She wrote primarily on science and was in the process of applying to graduate programs in science journalism in the U.S. Science writing wasn't that big yet, but Renuka believed that it had a future. After all, India was finally making technological advances, with its own satellites in space, even though the local phone system was not particularly reliable. Science writers would soon be in demand to explain new developments and breakthroughs to the public.

Gulnar stubbed out her cigarette and said: "I would rob the bank Geet used to work for. I know everything about it."

"It wouldn't work," said Renuka, surprised by her own words. Why was she going along with this?

"It would work. Nobody would suspect us. And I'm telling you, I know that bank inside out."

The waiter took their order – club sandwich, vegetable cutlets and prawn curry rice. Tanya had ordered one of the expensive items on the menu. She could afford to since she lived at home with her widowed mother. This also made it possible for her to be a theatre critic.

On weekends, Tanya conducted tarot card readings in her house, a venture that could have earned her some money, if she had treated her hobby like a business. But she did not concern herself with money, and her customers usually ended up owing her, or paying in kind. Stainless steel pots, statues of the Madonna with the infant Jesus, imported cosmetics, books on Marxism, awkwardly embroidered tablecloths, ugly photo frames and leaky plant holders had thus made their way into the Trivedi residence. Tanya did have the practical sense to give away some of the items as gifts to her cousins who were rapidly getting married and having babies. If Gulnar put art before life, Tanya reserved that spot for the Tarot.

"We would go in just before one o'clock, because the place would be closed to customers after that," said Gulnar. "That way we would deal mostly with the employees. And we would be incognito, of course."

"What the hell are you talking about?" said Tanya.

"The bank robbery," Gulnar said evenly.

"How would we be in-cog-nito?" Renuka found herself holding her breath.

"We would wear *burqas*," Gulnar responded triumphantly.

"You're assuming that we would all be involved," said Tanya.

"Naturally."

The trio had come together at St. Xavier's College. Tanya and Gulnar were enrolled in the B.A. Program;

Renuka in the B.Sc. They already knew each other when Renuka met them at a party. She had noticed them soon after she had come in, because they were dancing together, ignoring the considerable attention they were getting from the boys. Renuka stood in a corner nursing a rum and Thumbs Up, admiring the way they moved – Tanya with total abandon, Gulnar with controlled confidence. Renuka had come to the party with a friend who seemed to have disappeared. She was trying to decide if it would be better to go home, when Gulnar came up to her and asked her to join them on the dance floor. Renuka demurred.

Tanya joined them, a bottle of rum in her hand. She poured a liberal shot into Renuka's glass and gave her a wink. Renuka started loosening up after that, though she could not bring herself to dance for some time. Finally, when she joined them on the floor, she enjoyed moving to the frenetic disco beat more than usual. Soon after, Gulnar suggested that they move on to another party. After a couple of hours at the second, wilder party, they drove to Chowpatty beach in a jeep, with friends Gulnar had met there. Whenever the memory came up, Renuka could taste the ice cream she had eaten there – Tutti Frutti. She had never been on a beach that late, eating ice cream, giggling at everything. She was hung over the next day; but enveloped in a feeling of radiant elation.

After that the three of them had met practically every day, at the college canteen, after finishing their lectures. They had known each other now for five years. Renuka believed that she would never know anyone as well as she knew Tanya and Gulnar, not even her husband.

"What will you do with the money?" Tanya asked.

"Go to Singapore," Gulnar said. "Geet's going there for a conference in a couple of months. Or may be we'll all go to Bali."

"Why not China?" Tanya said. "I've always wanted to go there."

"Let's go China!" Gulnar said, leaning forward, her eyes gleaming.

After saying goodbye to her friends, Renuka walked briskly towards the State Bank of India, which was just down the road. She wanted to cash the money order her father had sent. Then she would pay the fees for her GRE Preparatory Course. The rest of the money would go to the American Express Bank for a dollar cheque, which she would mail to the U.S. to register for the GRE.

Go to China, Renuka thought. How impractical. Just the sort of thing Gulnar would think of, and Tanya could always be persuaded. Or it could work the other way around; the crazier the idea the better. How had she ever got involved with these two?

Despite their silliness, she was lucky to have them for friends. They were family to her here, in Bombay. Tanya's mother invited them for dinner from time to time and so did Gulnar's aunt, Kusum Vaid-Chopra.

Renuka recalled the first time she had gone to Kusum Vaid-Chopra's penthouse apartment at Kemp's Corner. The table had been laden with dishes and she was tempted to stash away some of the delectable *batata wadas* for lunch the next day. Her craving humiliated her. It would have made no difference to Gulnar's aunt. She had served a French wine at dinner, and Cointreau and imported chocolate mints on a silver tray, afterwards, in the spacious living room with its huge glass windows that looked down on the glittering city. The only other time Renuka had sampled such treats was at the French Food Festival at the

Oberoi Grand when Gulnar had bagged the assignment to review it for a glossy weekend supplement.

Renuka had been impressed by Bombay's glamorous façade when she had come here on a school trip as a teenager. She had insisted on studying outside Madras, even though her mother had been opposed to the idea. If she must go away, why far-off Bombay? Renuka had worked to get her father onside. Finally, their collective will had prevailed.

Exciting, quirky, dynamic – that was Bombay during her Bachelors. She had lived downtown then, where both her hostel and her college were located. But the picture had gone from a flaming technicolour to a greying black and white when she had started working and moved to Mahim. Commuting every day in the overcrowded, second class compartment of the local train, living in the hot, musty PG which cost her an arm and a leg, the high price of everything, the cheap, restaurant food which tended to upset her system had all started taking their toll. Renuka's mother commented on how haggard she looked every time she went home. It was time she came back to Madras and got married.

Renuka's father did not comment. He expected Renuka to be in the U.S. by the following year. He hoped that she would find a job there after she finished her Masters. Then they would find her a good husband with a Green Card. There was no dearth of well placed, Tamilian Brahmin boys in the U.S.

Renuka walked into the State Bank of India. After taking a token from the clerk, she took a seat, waiting for the digital sign board to display her number with a loud ping.

Banks. Banks were grey, silent places with bland-faced people behind glass panels and gloomy, somewhat anxious customers waiting on the other side.

It's like a morgue, thought Renuka, perhaps because so much money lies inert in the vaults. She had a vague notion that the money circulated, was lent out, invested. But she did not understand financial transactions beyond the simplest exchange of money: getting and depositing a cheque, paying rent, buying something. Dullness descended over her when she entered a bank, as if she had left her brain outside the door. She glanced at the other customers. Their posture was slack, introspective. It would be easy to enter a place like this and hold it up. People would react like zombies and do what they were told. Renuka bit her lip at the errant thought. How could she let herself be influenced by Gulnar's nonsense?

Renuka's next stop was the old, decrepit building that housed Bright Future Classes. The lift was not working, so she climbed an ill-lit staircase with chipped steps, to the third floor. There were two people already in the queue. She unzipped her purse, wanting to be ready with her neatly filled out application form and the money. Her fingers searched the pocket where she kept her money and encountered a thin slit at the bottom. No! The newly painted, light blue walls of the room receded into the distance. The girl ahead of her was staring.

She showed the girl the bottom of her purse. The slit was straight, precise – the work of a pro.

"Someone stole her money!" said the girl excitedly.

Everyone looked at Renuka.

Renuka looked at the clerk who was in charge of registration. "What's the latest I can register?" She was surprised that her voice sounded plaintive rather than panicky.

"You can come next week," said the woman, her tone gentle. "Write your name and address down on a piece of paper. I'll keep a place for you."

"You should go to the police," the boy who had just finished registering said. "The station's just here, near Victoria Terminus. Do you know it?"

Renuka nodded. The fact that people were being kind, taking an interest, allayed her anxiety somewhat. She had felt so strange a minute ago.

Clutching the purse against her, she walked towards Victoria Terminus, moving blindly past pavement shops selling books, cosmetics, toys, clothes, electronic items – the world. This had never happened to her in all the five years she had lived in Bombay. It had never happened to her, ever. How could it? How could it happen now? What would her father say?

Her father kept a neatly organized folder of her articles and showed it to all the visitors who came to their house. He had always told her to study hard, to enter a profession. He had bought her a series of illustrated books entitled *How Things Work* when she was a little girl in pigtails. He had offered to pay for all the GRE expenses, though he was so careful with money. Tight-fisted, her mother called him.

Mustard yellow envelopes from U.S. universities had winged their way to Renuka's PG every month. They were so strong, not like the shit-coloured, Indian ones that ripped easily. Inside were glossy brochures featuring smiling students in midstride, framed against expanses of green space, or sleek, modern buildings. The dream of an American University that she had lived with for months seemed elusive now. But no, she would not let go of it so easily. Perhaps the police would find the money?

The police station with its stained, peeling walls did not inspire confidence. Renuka gathered an impression of confusion and lethargy. There were several people waiting – poor, desperate-looking people, nothing like the customers at the bank.

Renuka looked around, then walked up to the most efficient looking person in the room. "M.J. Jadhav, Sub Inspector," said his badge. Sub Inspector Jadhav sat behind a simple wooden table on which lay an open file full of handwritten pages. Renuka introduced herself as a journalist. At first she had been reluctant to take advantage of the status her work gave her. Soon she had come to the realization that it was one of the few perks of the profession.

Inspector Jadhav asked her to write out a First Information Report. Did she recall anyone bumping into her or brushing by her after she had left the bank? No, not really, she said, in Hindi. Then she asked him what the chances of apprehending the thief were. Jadhav was non-committal.

"It's very important." *Damn it*, she wanted to add, but did not.

"Money is always important, madam," he said softly. He was a small-built, youngish chap with a thin moustache and warm, brown eyes. Without his uniform, Renuka would have never imagined that he was a policeman. She found herself pouring out her story of the GRE exam and the cheque from home. Jadhav listened sympathetically.

"They are very clever, these pick pockets," he said. "They often wait outside banks. They tend to operate in teams. If you had lost a watch or a chain ... we find things like that sometimes. But money ... Of course, we'll try our best."

Renuka stood indecisively outside the police station, blinking in the glare of the afternoon sun. There was not much more she could do. The money was gone. A little girl in ragged clothes touched her arm. Renuka shook her head; she had nothing for a beggar today. She had to talk to someone. Maybe Tanya would be home.

Tanya's mother answered the phone. "Tanya will be home late, after the play. You're going, no?"

Renuka remembered that they had fixed up to meet at Prithvi Theatre that evening. Tanya had got them complimentary tickets for a Hindi adaptation of *Hamlet*. Renuka's favourite actor, Nasiruddin Shah, was playing the lead role.

She reached the theatre a little before eight; Gulnar arrived a few minutes later. Renuka had decided not to say anything about the money till after the show. But one look at her face and Gulnar knew something was up. Renuka was recounting the story when Tanya arrived.

"Oh you poor girl!" Tanya threw her arms around her.

"You must call your father at once," Gulnar said. "Tonight."

"I can't! I can't tell him what happened. He'll be so upset. He'll ... shout."

A flush rose on Renuka's cheeks. She was wrong to expose her father like this. He wasn't normally hot tempered, but he flew into a rage sometimes.

"Tell you what, let's just talk," said Gulnar. "It'll be nice on the beach."

Renuka looked gratefully at her. The idea of a closed, dark theatre held no appeal. They would hook up with Tanya after the play.

Gulnar and Renuka walked down the sandy, tree-lined lane that led to Juhu beach. The palm trees made a rustling sound as they passed under them. The same light breeze that played with the fronds brushed against Renuka's face. Beyond the strip of sand was the inky, black sea at high tide, a bright line of white foam commemorating the union of water and land. Renuka, who had grown up by the sea, was glad to be near it. Her treacherous present had held her captive in the last few hours. She had lived almost entirely inside her own mind, which felt as constrained as her little room. The presence of the dark, undulating sea beyond the dimly lit beach, stretching out to the horizon, brought some relief.

"I would have asked Geet to lend you money," said Gulnar. "But he just blew his savings on a music system."

"I wouldn't take money from him."

"But you have to get money from somewhere. Kusum aunty could do it. It's 3000 rupees, isn't it?"

"I can't take money from her."

"Why not? You know it's nothing for her. You can return it whenever."

Never borrow money, Renuka's parents had always told her.

"Let's go to Fisherman's Rest," said Gulnar.

Gulnar was such a good soul, Renuka thought. She gave up the play for me just like that.

Sand seeped into her new sandals as they walked. Most of the money she had would go towards her rent, which was due in two days. She was expecting a couple of small cheques. Even if she scrimped on food she would never have 3000 rupees. She was hand to mouth as usual. She tried so hard to save, but it was no use. New expenses always cropped up – a birthday present, or a table lamp or alarm clock that needed repair. Or they would have a night out and she would be forced to take a cab home.

They found a table at the restaurant and ordered cold drinks.

"I'm sick of being broke," Gulnar said.

"Really? You don't seem to mind."

"I do. I would like to treat Geet sometimes. I give him little things, and a nice gift on his birthday. But it's not enough."

Renuka looked at her friend, surprised. She had envied Gulnar sometimes. She had everything – a devoted boyfriend, supportive parents who sent her a cheque to get her through a tight spot, and most of all, her devil-may-care attitude.

"And my parents. I would like to give them something too. Take a *saree* for Ma when I go home."

"I'm sure they understand," Renuka said. "You'll be able to do these things when you're more settled."

"That'll never be," Gulnar said emphatically. "If anything I may be poorer when I start writing my novel. I'll have less time for freelancing."

Renuka looked out at the sea. There were so many options in life. That's what she had believed as a child. And even in college, the world had beckoned her as a place full of promise. Where had she gone wrong?

"I have always admired you," Gulnar said. "I have no self discipline with money. I see an interesting book and I'm gone ..." She shook her head and took out a cigarette.

"You know my weakness. Asimov and Kurt Vonnegut. It's no use trying to save. I'm broke anyway."

"What you gonna do?"

"Don't know," Renuka said. She had been thinking and thinking, but there really did not seem to be a way out.

"You have to do something. Can't you tell your mother?"

Renuka shook her head. She didn't want to worry her parents. They had done so much for her already. She had to find a way out on her own.

Gulnar dropped her voice: "What about the bank idea?"

Renuka stared at her, incredulous.

"It's a one-shot deal. This bank I have in mind has 2.5 lakhs worth of cash transactions everyday. That's an average."

Gulnar paused to see how Renuka was taking it. Renuka looked away and took a sip of her Fanta.

"That sounds like a lot, I know," Gulnar continued. "But it isn't really. It's enough to give us some peace of mind. That's all."

Renuka emitted a hoarse, snorting laugh; she didn't associate peace of mind with bank robberies.

Gulnar smiled. "I've been thinking about it for quite some time. It was like a game for me – what if? It's not so much about our money problems right now, don't you see? It's for the future."

"We'd get caught," said Renuka matter-of-factly.

"That's what you think because of crime novels and movies. People want to believe that those who step out of line get punished. But they don't always. There are many unsolved crimes. Really. There are."

"What about Tanya?"

"She needs money. They've wanted to get their flat renovated for a long time. It's such an old building, you know that."

The whole thing is ridiculous, Renuka thought. Gulnar should have been an actress or novelist. I should have been in a journalism program in the U.S.A. It's all wrong and screwed up. Terribly, irreversibly wrong.

Renuka got home well after midnight. She was so tired that she had to pull herself up the stairs with the aid of the banister, one step at a time. She was out of breath by the time she got to the second floor. The evening had split her into two people: the Renuka who was going along with Gulnar's outrageous scheme - a shadow with a motive; and the Renuka who was still painfully embedded in her own flesh. The one had watched the other all evening, stifling a scream of horror and disgust.

The split had occurred at the precise moment Gulnar had pulled out a writing pad from her bag and started sketching out the layout of the bank. By that time Tanya had joined them and ordered a round of beer. Here was the entrance, Gulnar had shown them; here the windows; this was where the teller sat; here was the second exit in this room at the back. This was the moment when Renuka should have laughed, protested, maybe even slapped Gulnar. But she had not done any of those things. Her shadow self had taken over, listening to Gulnar's plan without judgment or emotion.

Tanya was to go and buy the *burqas* from Mohammed Ali Road. She was to go there after dark, wearing her large sunglasses, her head covered with a scarf. Gulnar was going to procure the revolver. Her uncle, Kusum Vaid-Chopra's husband, had one. It was kept in a locked drawer, but she knew where the key would be. Gulnar had found all this out quite by chance, she said. She was going to borrow the revolver, without telling anyone of course, for 24 hours. They were not going to load the gun. Gulnar was confident that it would not come to that.

Renuka was the one who would issue the commands, because she was a good mimic. It would be easy for her to change her voice. Gulnar was known to some of the bank employees because Geet had worked there for a year. Tanya's voice was deemed too feminine. The robbery would take 15 to 20 minutes. They would down the shutters as soon as they entered the bank. They would padlock it from outside, when they left. Since this would happen around the time the bank closed its doors to customers, it would not arouse suspicion. They would then take a rickshaw to the nearest cinema hall, go into the ladies room, whisk off their disguises, and deposit them in a dump.

Renuka sat down heavily on her bed. She had no energy to change into her nightdress or brush her teeth. She wanted to topple over and fall asleep that instant. But her mind kept spinning, a spider propelled by instinct. She knew that her two friends were wilder than her, much more capable of extremes. She was the steady one who wanted a good job, savings, and the chance to study abroad. She wanted to get married and have children. Being with Tanya and Gulnar made her life spontaneous, indulgent, fun. Sometimes their escapades scared her. Yet the things they had done in the past were harmless, with no real consequence. Renuka had gone along because she trusted her friends, believing that they would always look out for her.

A dog started barking somewhere on the street. Renuka lay on her bed, savouring the incredible comfort it brought to her exhausted body. Her friends were not to be trusted: they had divided her against herself.

She fell asleep. Or rather, she entered a beguiling unconsciousness from which she found it difficult to emerge next morning. When she came to, her landlady, Mrs. De Costa, was banging loudly on her door.

"Phone for you," she said, when Renuka opened the door. "Urgent."

It was 7:30 am. The only people who called her at that hour were her parents. Had her mother taken ill? She was diabetic. Renuka rushed into the hallway. It was Tanya, sounding very agitated.

She had woken up at dawn and done a Tarot Reading to get a handle on the situation. Sunrise and

sunset were powerful times in celestial terms because
they delineated night from day, dark from light. She
had opened the cards in the horseshoe format, which
was used for asking a specific question, rather than
for a general prediction. Her question had been: How
will it go?

The first card that had turned up was Temperance
and it had appeared upside down, signifying opposi-
tion created by ineptitude and a loss of balance. It
referred to the circumstances that had led to their
actions. It made sense. The lost money, the scheme
they had hatched, which was, after all, an extreme
measure.

Temperance was followed by the Hanged Man, a
card Tanya detested, even feared. It was a card signifying a giving over to inner drives, a reliance on
instinct rather than reason. One of Tanya's clients
had taken an overdose of sleeping pills a couple of
days after a reading in which the Hanged Man had
turned up. The man had been under treatment for
depression.

The card that indicated the probable outcome
of the scheme was negative as well. The Seven of
Swords indicated that the person was involved in a
plan that might fail. But the Seven of Swords was not
what upset Tanya. It was the Hanged Man. She had
not come upon that card for some time. Why now?
What did it mean?

Renuka pleaded tiredness, suggesting they talk
later. She found that she was shivering a bit when she
returned to her room, though it was a warm day. Her
brain felt foggy, so she decided to sleep some more.

When she woke up, Mrs. De Costa was knocking
on the door again. This time it was Gulnar calling to
see how she was.

"What do you mean?" Renuka said brusquely. "I'm not ill."

"Well, Tanya's quite upset. All this mumbo jumbo. Thank God you don't believe in the Tarot."

"No," Renuka said without conviction.

It was the first time Tanya had gone into such details about a Tarot reading. She knew that her two friends were born skeptics, and had never tried to convert them.

"I think we should all keep our heads," Gulnar said. "That's important."

Typically Gulnar! First she got them going, than she advised them not to get worked up.

Renuka started to come alive again as she stood under the shower. There was a new show at the planetarium, which she had to cover for *Science Today*.

In the imposing darkness of the planetarium as she watched millions of electronically projected stars transform the curved roof into the night sky, Renuka found herself thinking of the Tarot. How easy it was to fool the human eye! She and Gulnar rejected the Tarot because the reasoning behind it was not based on science, on something that could be proved, or disproved, through experimentation and repetition. But what was real, and what was its obverse? Last night she had become a shadow of herself. Gulnar had slipped into the fantasy role of a bank thief. Tanya's client had died after the Hanged Man had turned up at a reading.

On the double-decker bus home, suspended above the multi-layered animation of the city, she wondered about her dream of America. How had it become so real that she was ready to go along with Gulnar to attain it? She, Renuka Rao, science writer, was going to become a bank robber clad in a *burqa*? She had the sketch of the bank's layout in her bag. She was supposed to memorize it and pass it on to Tanya. She wanted to laugh hysterically, but ended up instead with the hiccups.

Renuka spent the evening writing her report. It was due first thing the next day. Then she sat down to the dinner of *sol-kadhi,* rice and *bhindi ki bhaji* that her landlady had prepared.

"Not feeling well?" asked Mrs. De Costa, watching Renuka pick at her food.

"I think I'm getting a cold," Renuka said, lying. "Just need a good night's rest."

Mrs. De Costa nodded sympathetically. She was the perfect landlady, solicitous without being interfering.

Leaving her and her two children watching TV, Renuka returned listlessly to her room. She sat down on her bed, and then reached impulsively under it to pull out the files where she kept her clippings. There were three separate folders. The red one had the serious articles she had written for *Science Today* and a couple of more scholarly magazines. The black folder held the intermediate pieces such as reports about the latest medical discoveries, a critical look at the concept of IQ and so on. She kept her frothy monthly column, published under the byline Madame Curry – an allusion to Marie Curie – in the blue folder. Tanya had come up with the name in one of her inspired moments.

The column consisted of rewrites of news stories from foreign newspapers: U.F.O. sightings in Nevada, explanations of right brain vs. left brain activity, vignettes about the mate-devouring, black widow spider. The sad truth was that Madame Curry's brand of pseudo science was more popular than Renuka Rao's well-researched articles explaining the difference between nuclear fission and fusion, with elaborate diagrams.

She started reading randomly from the articles, smiling. She had never read her articles after they were printed. The race was to get them done. Her byline always gave her a kick. But she had not looked back, only forward, to the next story. She read on, feeling pleased.

Suddenly a shadow seemed to enter the room. Renuka looked up uneasily. The curtain was swaying slightly in the breeze. No, there was no one there. But her hands felt clammy and her head heavy. She was on a downward slide, despite all the work she had accomplished. She could feel the undertow that would draw her down even further. Renuka put the files away and climbed into bed. She lay under the covers, looking at the ceiling, trying to transform it into the roof of the planetarium, but it remained resolutely blank.

There was a knock again. She was startled to see her father standing at her door. Mrs. De Costa hovered in the background.

"I tried to call but the phone's dead it seems," he said.

"Went off in the evening," Mrs. De Costa said.

Renuka found her voice. "Come in Appa."

"Are you well?" asked her father stepping in.

"She's getting a cold," said Mrs. De Costa.

"Too much running around," said her father.

"Would you like some tea?" Mrs. De Costa asked.

"No thanks. I just had dinner."

Mrs. De Costa left, satisfied that she had done her duty.

Her father surveyed the room. Thank God I'm tidy, Renuka thought. She pulled up the only chair in the room for him and sat down on the bed.

"My company had some work here," her father said. "My junior was supposed to come, but I decided to come myself. We tried calling you last night but couldn't get through."

It was strange to have her father there. Somehow, it changed the room. Her mother had come with her to Bombay to get her admitted to college, and settled into a hostel, years ago. But her life here was her own, a life totally different from her parents' or her earlier life, in her parent's home.

"You got the cheque?" her father asked.

Renuka nodded.

"Paid the fees?"

Renuka hesitated, than nodded again. The evening stretched ominously before her. She had never lied to her father with such impunity. The room felt like a trap, which had closed around both of them.

"Good," said her father, a broad smile lighting his somewhat severe face, lined with age. Suddenly she was aware that most of his hair had turned grey. Surely that hadn't been the case when she had seen him last time?

"Oh, I was forgetting. Your mother sent you something."

He gave Renuka a plastic bag. Inside was a beautiful, black, white and red, *kanchi* cotton, *salwar kameez*. Renuka gasped with delight.

"There's more," said her father, grinning like a schoolboy.

Renuka pulled out packets of food – *murukku*, gunpowder and some *laddus*. She looked at her father, on the verge of tears.

"Your cousin Vasanti is getting married in May. It was finalized just two days ago. Your mother's looking forward to seeing you then."

Renuka looked down at the packet of *murukku* in her lap. It was her favourite snack. She pictured her mother in her kitchen, making the dough, heating oil, shaping the dough into spirals and then frying the *murukku*. Tears ran down her cheeks, blurring her father's concerned face.

The next day, Renuka met Gulnar and Tanya on the steps of the Jehangir Art Gallery. They walked up to the terrace and sat down under the shade of a flowering Gulmohar tree. It was hot, but at least they had some privacy there.

"I'm very happy today," Gulnar announced. "I finally realized last night who Mallika is." She paused for dramatic effect.

"What?" Tanya said, looking confused. "You mean the heroine of your novel?"

"Yep," Gulnar said. "You know how I had always imagined that Mallika was born and brought up in Bombay? Her parents owned a restaurant? Well, I was on the wrong track. She is not from Bombay. If you've always lived here, it's no big deal. But if you're an outsider, you have to work to become a Bombay Wali. Know what I mean? You have to learn about the city. You have to learn about survival. It suddenly came to me last night. It was so exciting! I've even started on the first chapter."

"How wonderful!" Tanya said.

"My heroine is now modelled after you, Renuka. Sort of, anyway."

Renuka beamed. She did feel like a heroine, for the first time in her life.

"I was just with my father," she said. "We went and paid the fees for the GRE Class and then we got the dollar cheque. And we mailed it at the GPO."

Her friends gaped at her. She had caught them by surprise, for once. "I told him everything. He was very nice about it. Very nice."

Tanya started laughing, then Gulnar, then Renuka. Their laughter spread past the Jehangir Art Gallery

and The Wayside Inn, Bombay University's Rajabhai
Tower, over V.T. station, Kusum-Vaid Chopra's apartment at Kemp's Corner, over the Nehru Planetarium
at Worli, past Dadar to Mahim, Bandra, and the
Prithvi Theatre in Juhu, and went on, rolling over the
slum-speckled City of Gold, to Versova and Marve,
to mingle with the azure waters of the Arabian sea.

Middle Age Jazz
and Blues

Feroza Billimoria sits at her antique desk diligently marking history exams. Suddenly, there's a horrible twitch in her lower back. Letting go of her trusted, red ink pen, she moves her hand to rub the spot. The sharp pain quickly subsides, leaving behind a dull throb.

Her gaze rests momentarily on the faded, rather dusty poster, which hangs low on the wall before her. It depicts Lord Robert Clive meeting Mir Zafar after the Battle of Plassey, 1757, in Bengal, India. At this "decisive" battle, the British East India Company easily defeated the large army of Siraj-ud-daulah, Nawab of Bengal, because some of the Nawab's top officials had already struck a deal with the British. The poster is one more edifying wall decoration put up decades ago by her father, Hoshang. He had been forced to become an accountant, though his first love was history.

With her hand still on her lower back, Feroza looks down to see blood being spilt over a none too intelligent answer written in a beautiful hand by one of her more indifferent pupils. She seizes the pen. Now the ink starts staining her fingers. Capping the pen hurriedly, she puts it down on the stone floor.

She will have to use a ballpoint, she thinks, as she heads for the bathroom. At least till this pen is repaired, or she buys a new one. Perhaps she should switch to ballpoints. How often had her colleague, Piya, teased her about it, suggesting that she give up her ink pen and enter the 20th century?

To reach the bathroom Feroza must traverse a cavernous apartment on Marine Drive, full of old things, ancient really. The furniture, the books, the pictures, the crockery, the linen, the carpets, the records, the gramophone, the telephone, the knick knacks, everything here is old. Everything. Everywhere there is a scent of decay that cannot be dislodged, certainly not by the ineffectual efforts of their cleaning lady, who is also old. All things here belong to Papa – reflect his taste, or that of his father and grandfather. And a few, fussy, little things belong to mama.

At 90, papa still stands straight and walks tall, though his hand shakes a bit when he lifts one of the fine china teacups he has inherited from his ancestors to his thin lips. He pretends to hear everything, though he has gradually lost much of his hearing, particularly over the last five years. Mama, Mrs. Khorshed Billimoria, is a dwindling 85-year-old, wafting through the house draped in white *sarees*, pale and silent as a ghost.

Feroza opens the bathroom cupboard and takes out a tiny bottle of Tiger Balm. Such a potent remedy lurks in this innocuous looking container, she thinks. Over the years she has massaged the balm into the various aching parts of her parents. And now, already, it is her turn! Forty seven? Can I really be 47, Feroza muses. It does not seem real. It does not seem right.

Returning to her desk, she starts marking again. The phone startles her with its ring. It is Piya, telling her that her driver has not shown up, and they will have to leave for the Jazz Yatra earlier.

"I will pick you up at 7:30 sharp," she says. "Parking's going to be a nightmare."

"Fine," says Feroza.

"What are you going to wear?"

Feroza has not thought that far ahead. "Don't know yet."

"Why don't you wear your turquoise blouse and black pants?"

So, Piya is telling her how to dress! This is too much.

"Tie your hair in a high ponytail," Piya continues. "A few locks of loose hair create a soft look. And wear your pearl drop earrings."

"Let's see," says Feroza. Piya's fashion advice is rather good.

"Just trying to help, sweetie. You are such a brain, but you don't pay enough attention to your clothes sometimes. Don't mean to put you off."

How like Piya to issue commands, then toss in a half-hearted, conciliatory remark.

All the same, she comes away from the phone feeling light hearted. It's alright for Piya to advise me, she thinks, though she could use a less dictatorial tone. Feroza has known her for more than two decades, a trusted colleague who helps her navigate the murky world of college politics. She had forgotten to mention the back pain. Piya would have told her to pop a painkiller and come anyway.

Feroza is looking forward to the Yatra, a glamorous, bi-annual event, with Indian and international bands, where people go to be seen. She's never been before and was surprised when Piya asked her. It turned out that Piya's husband had to go out of town suddenly, on business. Oh well, at least she's going.

She hardly goes out, and rarely for late-night events. She goes to dinner parties given by aunts, uncles, cousins and family friends, but that's not really going out. What she enjoys much more is going for walks along the Marine Drive, and sometimes further afield, or going to the movies, followed by *chaat* and tea, on Sunday afternoons, with her cousin Arnaz.

She has not yet told mama and papa that she is going to the Yatra. She must do it at lunch.

A silent something seems to hang in the air when she returns from the infrequent night out. Perhaps it's a wisp of disapproval. Her mother seems to cough more this night and her father appears more frail the following morning, asking Feroza to bring his reading glasses and the newspaper to him, as he sits at the dining table, drinking his first cup of tea.

Parents want the best for their children, and certainly hers are exemplary in that regard. They had never nagged her about being single and tried to force her into an arranged marriage. Not once. That had been the fate of so many of her college friends. Feroza had not been averse to meeting suitable boys presented by her parents or siblings. There had been a few suggestions from her aunt, Coomi, Arnaz's mother. While looking for a groom for Arnaz, she had kept Feroza in mind as well. But for one reason or another, nothing had come of these efforts, and both Feroza and Arnaz remained single.

There were hardly any good Parsi men to be found anymore, her mother had often lamented. The best ones went abroad. The better ones among those left behind either wanted to remain bachelors, for some strange reason, or were quickly snapped up. Good thing Meher, her sister, had lucked upon one good candidate. Well, Meher was smart-looking and lively,

Khorshed would say, but Feroza ... Sighing tragically, she would raise the edge of her saree to her eyes, to wipe away a tear, real or imagined, then turn back to the TV or her rosary.

Her parents love her dearly, there's no doubt about that. From an early age, her father had taught her history and brought her endless Amar Chitrakatha comics featuring heroes from the Independence Movement. How proud they had both been when she passed her B.A., History Honours, with distinction. She had done equally well in her M.A., and become a professor. Her parents had never raised their voice when speaking to her. Never.

It's understandable that they get a bit anxious when I'm not here, she thinks. I am the only one around. Farhad, her elder brother, is a busy surgeon in Liverpool, with two grown-up sons and an artist wife. Her elder sister, Meher, married to an army officer, never lived in Bombay after her wedding, and is a mother of two as well.

Mama and papa needed her, they needed her more with every passing day. It is not Meher or Farhad who can remind them daily to take their medicine and make sure their prescriptions are up-to-date. Mama has high blood pressure and Papa has survived a stroke. It is Feroza's job to look after the thousand and one domestic details that plague daily life. She is the one who gets the kitchen tap fixed when the faucet breaks, threatening a flood, who goes over the quarterly dividends her parents' secure investments bring in and deposits them in their bank accounts, who makes sure the servant cleans and cooks properly and gets her pay on time, who does the weekly groceries, that too without a car, who supervises the painters who whitewash their apartment every five years ... Sometimes it seems endless. But she really shouldn't complain. She has such a good family; she's lucky.

A few hours later Feroza is seated amongst a well-dressed, perfumed crowd, in the second row at the Jazz Yatra. She's all jazzed up too. She not only followed Piya's advice, she added her own touches as well – a light coat of blue eye shadow, a faint line of kohl pencil, some blush on and lip gloss – all presented to her a couple of years ago by a niece who lives abroad. She has applied perfume to the hollow in her neck, behind her ears and on the inside of her wrists. And as the final touch, she has put her thick-rimmed glasses into their case and tucked it in her little black purse. She can do without them today.

The silence that met her declaration at lunch that she was going out late that evening is a distant memory. Feroza feels unlike herself as she sits before the large, open-air, brightly lit stage that pushes back the dark, creating its own radiant, little universe. Large banners announce that a major tobacco company is sponsoring the event. The most striking image is that of Jazz Yatra '85, written in gigantic gold letters, on the velvety, black backdrop. In the middle, somewhat dwarfed by the size of the stage, the galaxy of lights, the large number of speakers, all stacked up, are five men, with various instruments – a guitar, another larger guitar or guitar-like instrument, a bass perhaps, a drum set, a flute, and what is that – a saxophone? She wishes she knew jazz better.

She decides against asking Piya, whom she has pleased so well by dressing up. There are bound to be programs somewhere. She will find one during the interval.

After a welcome speech and many acknowledgements from a perky MC, dressed in a smart blue suit, the band swings into action. At first they seem to produce only disconnected sounds. Rather strange, Feroza thinks. Nevertheless, she finds herself waiting expectantly for the next blast on the sax, or the next drum roll. Everyone seems to hold their breath during the pauses and the very air appears to tremble in anticipation. Soon the weird, almost discordant notes start to blend into something larger and more compelling, and waves of irresistible sound enfold Feroza in their embrace.

Pervez! Suddenly she is transported to a dark, plush auditorium with an orchestra playing a Brahms symphony. She is sitting beside Pervez, feeling him listening to the music with his whole being, the way he always does with classical music. Pervez. Pervez! Feroza's heart, gripped by a great, grinding, swirling pain, is as frenetic as the music.

And now the other musicians have stopped playing and the saxophonist is going it alone. He raises his instrument to the sky and blows as if his life depends on it. The sax bleats like a demented creature. It howls, whines, growls, producing the most alarming sounds Feroza has ever heard. She is so scared that she wants to block her ears; instead she sits transfixed in her chair.

Pervez. Pervez Mistry, Visiting Scholar, had walked into the Professor's Common Room at Elphinstone College five years ago, and turned Feroza's life upside down.

The other musicians join in again and the music mercifully mellows and smoothens. Soon, the band is playing their last number, displaying more riveting tricks. But this time Feroza knows what to expect and remains relatively calm.

"Encore, encore," screams the crowd, and the band ends with a restrained number.

Piya turns towards her, her face flushed. "That was really something!"

Feroza nods.

"You look … I don't know. Are you okay?"

Feroza nods again, unable to speak just then. Someone a couple of rows over calls out to Piya, and she turns away.

The next band is a 10-person swing ensemble making the kind of music Feroza has heard before. The melodious sounds free her mind and her thoughts turn towards Pervez. She should have known that she would be compelled to think about him at the Yatra! She shouldn't have come. She should have just stayed at home. But …

"You have to go on living. You have to. You must." She remembers Arnaz's emphatic words at the hospital, and how she had held on tightly to her hand, everyday, for many days.

She would think of him. She would allow herself to think of him now, even though she usually denies herself that. She would think of him, even though it still hurt very much.

Feroza's Prince Charming was a short, rather portly man in his early 50s, with a black goatee, lots of thick, black hair and small, sparkling eyes. His movements were quick, exhibiting the restless energy of someone half his age. He was one of those eligible Parsi bachelors who had settled in London. There was enough money in the family, so he did not have to work for a living, as long as he lived fairly simply. Pervez had chosen to devote himself to the study of history, and to teaching the occasional college course. He researched, wrote books, and travelled, using grants that he received fairly regularly. His next book was going to be about the taxation system in British India.

The somewhat impoverished Elphinstone College had decided to offer him a semi–voluntary, Visiting Scholar position for six months. They had promised him a room with a desk, access to the library, the opportunity to chair an international conference that was going to be held in Bombay, and not much else. Since Pervez could stay with his aging aunt in a spacious, Napean Sea Road apartment for free, he had accepted. He could have done all the research in England but he had a soft corner for Bombay, the city of his birth, which he had happily deserted in his early 20s, to study at Oxford. Since then he had only visited Bombay for family weddings and quick research stints. He liked the idea of a longer stay. He dreamt of watching cricket at the Wankhede Stadium, which was quite close to Elphinstone. There was cricket in London of course, but it came with a biggish price tag. He told himself that he missed the chaos and colour of India, and felt that he could enjoy it in Bombay, in a controlled manner.

Feroza was well into a part-time Ph.D. when Pervez appeared on the scene. They were introduced at the small reception that the Dean held to welcome Dr. Mistry. After that, they would run into each other in the hallowed hallways of Elphinstone College, and stop to talk, as noisy students streamed by. Soon Pervez suggested that she come by his work room where he kept some books that would surely interest her, and where they could chat more leisurely. Feroza wanted to go, she wanted to go desperately, but she held back. The college was a gossipy place; she did not want to set tongues wagging.

Then, one day, her mother told her to come home early and help with dinner, as they were expecting a Professor Mistry who was the son of one of her father's former classmates. Seeing Pervez in the chaste interior of her own home threw Feroza into a tizzy. But there he was, sitting in an overstuffed chair, smiling at her from time to time, smoking a cigar her father had offered him after dinner, very much at ease.

"What do you think of Feroza's thesis topic?" her father had asked Pervez. Feroza was studying the rise of the Bhakti Movement in 13th century Maharashtra.

"Very interesting," said Pervez.

"Really, you think so? Your area of study is much more solid."

"Perhaps," said Pervez in an even tone. "But hers is more original."

At that moment, Feroza fell in love with Pervez. She would have done anything for him. Anything. But he wasn't asking for much. Tea at a cafe on Napean Sea Road, dinner at the open-air restaurant at the Racecourse, a play or concert at the NCPA – these were the sorts of diversions that he invited her to, and she gladly went. She also visited him sometimes in his rather musty, little den at work now, though always discreetly.

She had finally met a man she felt at ease with. At the same time, she held him in awe. He knew so much! She was eager to learn. But she also had something to offer, her own ideas about history, which she had never shared with anyone else. And Pervez was receptive, he was engaged, as he looked at her with his dark eyes so full of life, and dare she hope, love?

She did not say anything to her parents. She had not gone out with anyone before and she didn't know how to tell them. And it wasn't time yet, she told herself. She had been a different creature back then, going out more, even at night, with Piya, Arnaz and other friends. Her parents were used to it, and did not ask for details. They had their own life then

— evenings at their Club playing bridge and visiting friends on weekends.

One day, in the auditorium at the NCPA, where they had gone to see a play, Pervez took her hand in his and caressed it gently.

"Sexy dress the girl is wearing, nai?" whispers Piya. Feroza realizes that the swing band is no longer there. Instead, there are four other musicians setting up. One of them is a tall, rather well built girl in a snug, black dress that goes to mid thigh and shows her light brown shoulders and some cleavage, through the sheer material that makes up the top. The girl holds a mike to her mouth, and with eyes half closed, sways lightly to the low, background music that is playing between the change of bands. Feroza nods.

She remembers Pervez's full lips and how his tongue had tasted when he kissed her, in the back of a cab, for the first time. He had gently brushed his lips against hers, then pressed them into her hair. He had proceeded to kiss her eyelids and moved back to her lips, kissing her deeply. It was the most intimate touch she had ever had and it penetrated to her core.

Music wafts down from the stage, and after a few riffs, the girl starts singing:

> *I don't know why but I'm feeling so sad*
> *I long to try something I never had*
> *Never had no kissin'*
> *Oh, what I've been missin'*
> *Lover man, oh, where can you be?*

"Oooooh, it's a Billie Holiday song I just love," Piya says. Feroza knows this number as well. She feels the prickle of tears and fights them the best she can. This is too much! She wants to flee, but how can she leave now?

> *The night is cold and I'm so alone*

I'd give my soul just to call you my own
Got a moon above me
But no one to love me
Lover man, oh, where can you be?

Tears flow down Feroza's cheeks, mussing up her make-up. She can feel a sob forming in her throat.

"Excuse me." She rises and makes her way between the chairs and legs, stumbling. Once free of her row, she practically runs to the nearby Clubhouse, conscious that quite a few eyes are on her. There is a wide veranda on the side, with a little recess in one corner. Stepping into shadow, head against a wall, finally alone, she weeps, and weeps some more.

Pervez had asked her to accompany him on a field trip, to a fort not too far from Bombay, but far enough that it meant an overnight stay. It wasn't part of his research. It was just a get-away. He had seen the fort before and now he wanted her to see it, and take photographs.

Feroza was in an agony of indecision. She wanted to go, of course, but what could she say to her parents? Finally, she and Arnaz had concocted a lie. They had told Feroza's parents that they were going to Lonavala with some friends. But it was with Pervez that she went, in a hired car, over the Western *Ghats* and into an accident.

She should have died in the hospital. It was easy to die in a hospital with its grey walls, white clothed staff, hushed voices, bland food, and the faint smell of disinfectant trying to smother other smells, of urine, vomit, shit and offensive human excretions.

She had regained partial consciousness after two days, her mind in a haze, and asked about Pervez. He was no more, a nurse had told her. No more. She could still recall the perfectly oval face of that young nurse, and how it had receded from her vision as she mouthed those words. She had slipped back into unconsciousness, and tried to die. Lying for weeks on the narrow bed in her little, private room, not moving, not eating, not drinking. Hardly breathing. She had chosen to re-enter that lightless place, still as a crypt, somewhere deep inside her. She had been happy there, happy to be not quite a person, absolving herself of all decision and responsibility.

But she could not stay there forever. Sooner or later she had to leave. That much was clear. But where would she go? Up into the world with blank walls, lowered voices and smartly tapping feet on cold floors, or onwards to some other place, a place where Pervez had gone?

She wished she had believed in that other world. She had waited for a sign. Even the slightest indication would have swayed her. She did not need tunnels of light and disembodied voices calling to her. Something far more subtle could have edged her on. But she had got nothing, nothing at all.

But from the world that she already knew, she felt presences, and heard voices, at first indistinct. Her father, mother, sister, nephew and niece, Piya, her aunt Coomi, other relatives and friends were there. It seemed that even some of her students stood sometimes by her bed. Fleetingly, she had sensed her brother and sister-in-law's presence. And most of all, there was Arnaz, who came every day, sat by her bedside and spoke to her, described the flowers she had got her, spoke of what was happening in the family, in the city, held her hand tightly and urged her back. At first her voice was muted, but it got stronger and clearer, until Feroza could no longer ignore it.

"You can't give up. You have to go on living. You must." Arnaz's words had started echoing in her consciousness, had acquired a force all their own.

And so she went on living. After weeks in limbo, she relinquished the crypt and entered a world full of blinding light and deafening sound.

Then began the protracted journey back, through a swirling dust of incomprehension and denial and pain. Pain: black, sticky, unrelenting. How murky life had seemed to her then, during those first months, and beyond. It was as if reality was obscured by a ring of pale, barely perceptible dust, which kept her off balance and unsure. She had confided at last in Arnaz, afraid that perhaps she was losing her mind.

It had been easy to turn to Arnaz. Arnaz, just a year older, with whom she had grown up. She felt closer to Arnaz than to her sister or brother. Arnaz had consoled her, told her to take long walks, go slow, spend time by herself, cry when she needed to, and call on her anytime.

Feroza finds a none-too-clean bathroom and washes her face. She stands for a few moments by the Clubhouse wall, looking at the stage a little way off. The blues band is still on. Feroza feels herself moving slightly to the beat. She had better go back and apologize.

When she gets back, it is Piya who is full of whispered apologies, offering to take her home right away.

"I am all right now," Feroza says. "Really."

She sits through the rest of the performance, calm, enjoying it from a distance. She is outside the music now, a spectator taking in the show, not a being engulfed by it.

On the drive back, Piya starts apologizing again, but Feroza cuts her short.

"I am glad I came," she says. "Thank you, Piya."

Relieved, Piya drives on in silence.

"Sleep well sweetie," Piya says as Feroza exits the car. "Take tomorrow off."

Feroza waits for Piya to drive away. Then, instead of taking the stairs to the apartment, she walks away from the building, braving the stares of the security guard at the gate, and heads towards the sea face.

It is a balmy night, not very far from a full moon. Standing by the low wall that runs along this part of Marine Drive, Feroza looks beyond the rocks and sand, at the gentle sea. The sky is clear and shows a few stars. Cars swish by behind her. Someone strolls by occasionally, not paying her much attention. Looking at the sea has always had a beneficial effect on her, though she had not looked at it so late, so close, for many years.

She feels as if she has visited a garden with lots of beautiful plants, well-tended flower beds, tall trees and songbirds. She wonders: Where is all the swirling dust that made barren this place before? Now that it has cleared, here is a vision of peace and harmony. But where was it before? Was it always there, obscured, lost in the eye of the storm? Or did it come into being later? She has no answers, nor really the need for any.

Pervez is gone forever. But she is here. So is the sea, and mama, papa, Arnaz and hundreds of things that make up the world.

She feels calmer than she has in years. The Ph.D. was left undone, but she is still Professor Billimoria, with the responsibility of teaching history to undergraduates at Elphinstone College. Not all her students are uncaring. Sometimes there is someone like Suman, who wants to be an IAS officer, or Nikhil who wants to be a journalist. She has even taught a few who wanted to be historians.

Feroza stands by the sea, not quite looking at it. The shuffle of feet close by brings her back. As the person passes on, she looks incredulously at the inky, dark blue expanse. Here and there, near the shore, light glints off the surface. This sea stretches to foreign shores, she thinks. One can get on a ship and go to such places. Sail away to the coast of Africa, for instance. How unbelievable that seems, and yet it is true. It would be easier, though, to take a plane.

Taking a plane, just what Arnaz had suggested: a three-week, package tour of the Far East. The price was quite reasonable.

"But …," Feroza had said.

"I know, I know. You're thinking how will you leave aunty and uncle alone. Well, we could go in summer. Meher could come and stay. She's always saying she doesn't get enough time with them."

It could be done, with some effort all around.

Suddenly she's tired, very tired. With a last look at the sea, she turns and walks back to the building. She lets herself into the apartment very quietly, and gets into bed, after a minimal toilette.

A ray of moonlight comes in through a slit in the curtained window and touches her smiling face. Feroza is fast asleep, dreaming of distant lands.

The Tea Drinker

Her dress is a dazzle of white, her arm, a column of brown allure, her wrist delicate, her hand fine fingered, which I always see poised in mid-air, holding a teacup. Vapour rises from the cup, filled with the teas of the world. Or should that be tears of the world?

Oh, the many splendoured world of tea at The Britannia — Earl Grey, Lapsang Souchong, Oolong, Darjeeling. Tea flavoured with saffron, rose petals, jasmine and orange blossoms. Served in delicate china cups, white or pastel, sometimes with a gold rim, sometimes imprinted with a floral pattern, a pastoral scene, or a ship a sail.

All this and more did Manny Kaplan export to the island to woo tourists to his teahouse — British, Spanish, French, Germans, Italians — the wealthy off-spring of former colonizers.

Sometimes I go to a teahouse in Toronto, even though I can ill-afford the three dollars and fifty cents for a cup, tax and tip extra. Every so often I glimpse a woman in a fashionable pair of sunglasses and a broad-brimmed straw hat, dark hair descending to her shoulders. I feel my senses quicken. Then she turns, and my hope dissipates, a sugar cube in hot liquid, leaving behind a slight residue.

I can't relate to the Toronto teahouse. I, Martin Danilo, in this faux Japanese interior. It feels fake.

But I go anyway because from here I can travel easily to The Britannia, enter it through the white-painted, wooden doors that always stood open and welcoming, sit down under the perpetually rotating ceiling fan, languid yet purposeful, sense the presence of the sea – traces of sand on the floor, the faint, damp smell of seaweed, the sound of waves crashing in the distance.

How proud Manny was of his English teahouse! Of the painting of Queen Victoria on one wall, the black and white photograph of Sir Winston Churchill, the Navy memorabilia, the fussy china figurines of dogs, cats, accordion players and ballerinas, and all the paraphernalia that arrived at your table when you ordered tea – tray, teapot, tea cosy, strainer, coaster, cup and saucer, an elegant little silver spoon, milk container and sugar bowl.

I imagine Manny in his pokey little house, a glass of local whisky at hand, swearing over the imported magazines and catalogues, sweating over his account book, fearful that he would never get it right. As Manny fashions his atypical dream into reality, his wife Fancy cooks chicken, and the smell of fried onions, cloves and red peppers wafts out of the kitchen and tickles his nostrils.

Fancy did her bit to make The Britannia a success. She maintained a shrine to the local deities, in a curtained alcove in the kitchen. And every night at closing time, she would put a little food outdoors, to appease the hungry ghosts.

Dallying over such details, I finally come to Maliha. She is sitting in a wicker chair lined with cushions, at the corner table, alone, looking out of the window. She could sit very still; a stillness in her movements even when she drank tea, a minimalism that made one think of a statue brought momentarily to life.

We had just had dinner – my parents, my sister Darlene and my brother Trevor. My parents had gone into the living room. I was in the hallway trying to fix my bike when I heard my mother say: "Guess who washed up on shore?"

My father said nothing.

"Maliha," she continued.

"Really?" my father said. "Who told you?"

"She was at Manny's. He tried talking to her, but she got all high and mighty on him. Such a weird fish. Nothing good ever comes from mixing the races."

Maliha. I seemed to remember something about a girl with an island father and a British mother. Her story was known to the adults but not to us children.

A couple of days later I went to The Britannia. I used to run errands for Fancy, shelling and chopping cashew nuts, peering into containers to check on the flour or sugar levels, going to the grocery to make emergency buys. In exchange I got to sit at a table when the place was not crowded, eating Fancy's wonderful cakes – fragrant and fruity. Tucking in, I covertly observed the foreigners, taking in their gestures, the inflections in their speech, and the way they behaved towards each other.

At the teahouse I placed myself behind the large, well-stocked aquarium that I loved so much, and surveyed the scene. I spotted her right away. White dress, wide-brimmed, straw hat and large sunglasses – the standard costume of the white women tourists. But she was brown. Not sun-tanned brown, but real brown. Her features were neither foreign nor familiar but something in between. I stared, and stared some more. Then Fancy came into the passageway and asked me why I had not said hello.

A week later my mother reported that Maliha had rented the French-style villa in a quieter part of the island. I often passed by the house on my bicycle, on my way to a beach not far from the place. Not many people went to this rocky, windswept beach, where the land rose to form dunes, low cliffs and small, shallow caves. All the hotels were on the other side of the island with its picture-perfect beaches.

It was this beach that drew me and I had been exploring it for a couple of years. I liked to take a book to a cave, where I was protected from the glaring heat. I had learnt how to avoid the rocks and swim out to the tiny island that lay close to the shore. Here I would examine the plants that had made the difficult soil their home, observe small, burrowing insects and spot bird nests among the bushes. I had a favourite rock perch. Looking out at the sea as it stretched to infinity, I imagined being the prince of a fabulous kingdom at the depths of the ocean. I had long decided that I was a sea creature mistakenly cast into human form.

Two more weeks passed, and my mother announced that "she" had moved in.

"Didn't bring much furniture. Lots of books, paintings and a grand piano. All pricey stuff too."

"Likely she has taste," my father said laughingly.

"She can afford it."

Fragments of Maliha's story started floating in on the salt winds that traversed the islands and linked us to the rest of the world. I knew now that she was an heiress, having inherited the considerable fortune of her island father.

The next evening I took a detour coming home from school and found myself outside the lovely, two-story house. The small front garden had a lawn, a mini fountain, fruit trees and rose bushes. The house had lain vacant for over a year because the owner, who lived in Europe, was a picky landlord.

Now there were curtains on the windows and the ones downstairs were drawn back. The house stood on higher ground than the road, so it was difficult to look inside. I took to going by the cottage often.

It was already evening when I got there one day. As I paused in front of it and looked up at the lit windows, classical piano music drifted out, and tinkling, buoyant notes washed over my cooling skin. Suddenly, I felt illuminated from within. The fading light had a touch of gold and pink, and I had an acute sense of the vastness of the world, its strangeness, and an intuition that my life was going to change. I felt lightheaded and a bit reckless and pedalled furiously all the way home.

That Saturday afternoon, after a swim at the beach, I paused again before the villa. I watched for some time. Nothing moved. I had to sneak into the garden and take a peek at the living room. I was not a bold lad, not in the least. But I had to do it. In all likelihood Maliha was not at home.

I gently opened the garden gate, which made no sound. As I started walking up the path, a feeling of uncertainty seized me. I arrived at the porch in a state of fear and excitement that I rather liked.

I stood looking in on the few pieces of elegant, period furniture, a simple rug, a chandelier and some paintings. Then the side door swung open and I was face to face with Maliha.

Petrified, I looked into her grey-blue eyes for the first time. What an unusual colour they were! Fascination overtook fear. Her expression was striking as well. There was a note of absence, as if, even though she was looking right at me, part of her was somewhere else. Strange fish. No, a bird. She reminded me of a lost bird.

"Come in," she said easily, as if finding a 12-year-old boy peeking into her house was perfectly normal. "Have some lemonade. It's pretty hot, isn't it?"

The next thing I recall is being in her sunny kitchen, seated opposite her at a square dining table, a glass in hand. I kept my eyes on the yellow-patterned tablecloth, expecting questions. Adults always had questions.

But she said nothing for quite a while. I glanced up and found her looking out at the back garden, where vegetables grew in orderly plots.

She turned to me then and said: "What's your name?"

"Martin," I said.

"Good," she said, with a finality of sorts.

I came home that day with a picture book about jellyfish. She had asked me if I would like to borrow it. By then I had read practically all the books in the school library that had anything to do with the sea. I hid Maliha's book at the back of my cupboard. All library books were bound, labelled and easily identifiable. I didn't want anyone to know about this one.

I took to going to Maliha's house on Saturday afternoons. Sundays were out as they meant going to church, often followed by an elaborate dinner that involved aunts, uncles and cousins. Saturdays seemed to suit her too. There was no one around that day because her maid and gardener had the weekends off.

Gradually she asked me about school, my family, my hobbies. But conversation was not the centrepiece of our meetings. After she had given me a drink, sometimes a cookie, she would drift off to play the piano. I would stand by it and turn the pages of her music sheets. A couple of times she gave me a piano lesson. Sometimes she would go back to the book she was reading, while I leafed through her books or wandered around looking at the paintings. Sometimes I brought a book along. If I got restless I would go out into the back garden, admiring the amazing variety of vegetables and herbs that grew there. Sometimes we would sit in the kitchen, drinking tea and listening to the radio, which was always turned to a music show. Things fell into place at Maliha's house and the afternoons were perfectly companionable.

One day she asked me if I would like to read an adult book.

"Like what?" I asked.

She walked wordlessly to the bookcase and came back with *The Old Man and the Sea*.

"Try it," she said. "But don't read it if you don't like it."

I found it hard going at first; it was nothing like the abridged, English classics I was used to, nor an adventure series like the Hardy Boys. But I persisted and started caring for the old man and the boy and the fish. After I had finished it, I decided to read it a second time.

Sitting by my bedroom window, engrossed in the book, I didn't notice that my mother had come in.

"What's that book?" she asked.

"A library book," I said.

She came over to take a look.

"Where did you get that?"

I did not reply.

"Tell me Martin," she said.

There was no way out. "Maliha gave it to me."

My mother dragged me over to the drawing room, where my father sat reading the newspaper.

"There's something you should know," she said. "Martin's been going to that woman's place."

My father looked puzzled. My mother explained the situation.

My father took the book from me and looked at it.

"Have you been to Maliha's house?" he asked gently.

I stood silent.

"Come on, you can tell us," he persisted in the same tone.

I shook my head.

"Did she give it you at The Britannia?" he asked.

I nodded assent.

"There's no harm done," said my father, looking with some amusement at my mother. "She must have got talking to Martin. Got to know he loves reading and got him this book from her house. It's a good book, you know. A classic. Don't you remember? We had an excerpt from it in our Reader."

My mother merely pursed her lips.

"Don't go neglecting your studies," she said to me.

I nodded again. Retrieving the book, I made for my room. I was happy that I had won and my mother had lost. After that I was extra careful when I went to Maliha's house, always looking out for people.

Maliha was pleased that I liked the book. The next time I went to see her, she showed me her drawings.

They comprised of a few lines on a page: straight lines of varying lengths drawn at different angles, sometimes intersecting, sometimes not. Mostly black on white, but some pages had red or blue lines. A couple of the drawings featured shapes – triangles and circles. And one had wavy lines.

I did not understand them at all, though I found them intriguing.

I knew they were important to her by the way she handled them. So I looked at each one seriously, letting my eyes run along the lines without thinking of anything else. It made for a pleasing sensation. My response must have satisfied her, because she showed me new drawings from time to time. She mentioned once that she had studied under a famous artist in Paris for a few years. She named him, but it meant nothing to me.

She never talked of her past, yet it was with us in the living room, dominated by a large family portrait. I would often sneak a look at this oil painting. It showed a well-dressed, rather handsome, island man, her father presumably, who looked confident and relaxed. A smile played on his sensuous lips and reached his eyes. The mother was simply dressed, brown haired and blue eyed. She looked distracted. The girl in the picture was perhaps three years old. She looked like a younger version of Maliha, but her gaze was open and expressive.

Sometimes I reflected on the story behind the portrait, which I had come to know much better.

The son of a land-owning island family had courted a British woman who was holidaying in the islands. They had got married and lived together well enough for a few years. When Maliha was five, the mother had upped and left, taking the little girl with her. Rumour had it that a man from her mother's earlier life had landed on the island and enticed her away. This was before there were regular flights to the islands, and people took the five-hour ferry over from the mainland.

For the next ten years Maliha lived with her mother in England. Then the mother (apparently alcoholic and indebted) died, and her English relatives sent her back to the islands. Her father had remarried and she was not welcome. She was sent to a posh boarding school on the mainland. The school had a college, and Maliha continued her education there. After graduating, she taught at the school for some years. Then her father died, leaving his entire fortune to her. Why he disowned his second wife and son, the story did not say.

It was not clear what had happened next. It was rumoured that she had gone to Europe and lived there for some years. Then one day, she had reappeared on her father's island. Settling some money on her half-brother and stepmother, she had travelled around the islands, looking to rent a house.

Such a story, I think, sitting in the Toronto teahouse, such a story that it still defies my considerable imagination. The strange thing is, the fact that I can't really imagine her life, and what she went through, ties me to her.

My final exams were coming up, so I told Maliha that I would not be able to visit for a few days. She wished me luck and gave me a sleek, silvery pen, which I hid carefully in a box of old toys. I felt that even my father would not approve of this gift.

A week passed in the feverish, unreal manner of exam time. I only had my geography exam left. I had come downstairs to get a glass of water when I heard my parents talking in the living room.

"So she has a friend, I hear," my father said.

"Black, black as coal," my mother replied. "An American."

After my exam the next day, I went directly to her house. She was not in. I rode out to The Britannia and took up my position behind the aquarium.

They were at her usual table. He was black all right – big, black and old. Not coal black but a sort of greyish-black. My mother was wrong again.

They were talking intimately, oblivious to the surroundings. He said something and she threw back her head and laughed. He smiled then, his teeth a shock of white, and took her small hand in his large one.

I left right away and went to the beach. It was late afternoon and the shadows were beginning to lengthen. I chose the long, narrow cave and sat down, looking out at the blue haze of the sea. The image of Maliha laughing with her head thrown back kept returning. She had never done that with me. She rarely smiled.

I felt imprisoned, held down by a terrible weight that I could not budge.

There were black people on some of the other islands, but not on ours. We were all brown. The black people were poorer and I had gained the impression from what my mother and some of my relatives said that they were not as good as us. I had never really thought about it before. Now I decided that it was true. The blacks were inferior and Maliha had demeaned herself by associating with this man.

That was the easy part. The hard part was not knowing what to do with all the emotions that were surging so powerfully through me, emotions I could scarcely name.

When I got home it was dinnertime and my family was clamouring to know how the exam had gone.

I sat at the table, picking at my food.

"Overwork," my mother declared, running her hand through my hair. "Go to bed early today."

For once I took her advice. I lay in bed with a book, not reading, looking at the dark rectangle of the window.

Darlene came by a little later with a glass of warm milk. I drank it down; I was starving.

"Want a banana?" she asked.

I shook my head. She gave my hand a little squeeze.

"I'm sure you'll be better tomorrow," she said.

I was, and so my mother sent me out on an errand. I walked instead of biking. Just as I got out of the store, I ran into Maliha.

"Why Martin!" she exclaimed. "How are you? How did the exams go?"

I stood rooted to the ground, staring at her. This was not the Maliha I knew, but an odious stranger. Noticing my expression, she looked puzzled, then hurt.

"What's the matter?" she asked, holding out her hand.

I shrank back. Turning, I ran.

"Wait!" she cried out. "Come back, Martin."

I stayed home for the next couple of days. It was easy because my aunt Amy and uncle Charlie had came for a visit. Aunt Amy was my father's elder sister. They had been living in Canada for many years. A jolly man, I had always liked Uncle Charlie.

Soon after they left, we went on a holiday. The trip had been planned for some time and I was excited about it. It was my first holiday on the mainland, my first stay at a resort hotel with a swimming pool, an enormous buffet table and an amusement park nearby.

Somewhere during this happy time with my family, my feelings about Maliha changed, and in my mind she became the old Maliha again. I picked out some stones, unusually shaped and coloured, to take back to her as a gift. I decided that, when I saw her next, I would ask her to come climbing up the cliff with me. The locals never went there, so it was unlikely that we would be seen.

On our return we got the news that Maliha had locked up the house and left. No one was sure where she had gone. She had taken a late ferry to the mainland, alone.

Anguished weeks followed, weeks replete with guilt and shame. I was sure she had gone away because of me. How could I have behaved so badly? I forgot my reasons for judging her. I forgot the black man. All I knew was that I had been her only real friend. And she mine.

When I passed by her house, I looked up at the windows, hoping for a light to come on, praying for music to flow out and engulf me. But there was only darkness and silence. Her table at The Britannia also stood empty.

Maliha did not return. There was nothing, no news, no stories, no rumours. I had lost her forever.

But she had left something behind.

I had never really noticed paintings before, now I saw them everywhere. I studied the large, gloomy oils depicting hunting scenes at the Club, and the austere portraits of former principals at school. Covertly, as I knew that this activity would be considered strange. Seascapes sold in shops along the beach I looked at more openly. And I perused art books in the library.

Sometimes, at a family party, or an informal football game during recess, I would start thinking about how an artist might depict the scene, what angle she would take, what she may choose to highlight, and most importantly, what she would omit. This led me to think about how a writer would describe a particular event. I began to realize that it wasn't just an event that an artist or writer tried to capture but rather a mood, an emotion or a nuance. There was a connection between art and life that was as alive as a beating heart, yet it was indirect, tantalizing.

I finished secondary school and entered college. To my parents' disappointment, I decided to study political science. My brother had studied accountancy and played cricket on the university team. Darlene had pursued pharmacology at a college on the neighbouring island and got a job at a medical store. During my undergraduate years, Trevor got married and Darlene became engaged. I finished my B.A. and started working as an assistant to a local politician.

My eccentricities seemed to irk my parents more with the passing years. They commented when I had my head in a novel by Marcel Proust instead of going to the Club for a drink. Or when I skipped a football tournament where all the islands competed against each other to direct a play for an amateur theatre group. And when was I going to take a young woman out dancing?

They did not know of my affair with an older woman tourist that briefly sweetened my bookish life. We parted, not unhappily, when she went back to her husband at the end of four weeks.

The idea of leaving the islands had been growing on me for some time. Uncle Charlie's marriage had ended and his visits to the island were not very frequent, but we maintained a sporadic correspondence. I wrote him saying that I needed to get away. A few days later, he surprised me with a call.

"Put in your papers, Martin," was the first thing he said. "You can stay with me as long as you like. There's nothing for you there."

I wondered if it could be that simple. I went to see an immigration lawyer and told my family what I was considering.

My parents were instantly enthusiastic.

"A young man must travel," said my father.

"Look at Percy," said my mother. "Went to America, made his money, came back and is getting married next week."

Darlene took me aside later that evening.

"You are so different, Martin," she said quietly. "I think you'll like Toronto. There will be galleries, book stores and the theatre."

I laughed. "I will be too poor to afford them."

"You'll find your way," she said. Putting her hand on my shoulder she continued: "It's because of her, isn't it?"

It had been an unspoken rule in our house not to mention Maliha by name. Even after all these years, Darlene abided by it.

"No," I said, looking at my sister. "That was a long time ago."

Darlene looked relieved. "Look," she said, "if you don't like it, just come back. There will always be room at my house for you."

I pecked her quickly on her cheek and turned away. My eyes were moist and of course I did not want her to see that.

Now, in this marvellous city, Maliha accompanies me every morning on the ferry from Toronto to Toronto Island, where I have a temporary job at the Information Centre. She's there again on the evening ferry, her dress a dazzle of white, her arm — slim and brown — next to mine, not quite touching. We journey in a companionable silence tinged with a melancholy that is not unpleasing.

Maliha leaves me when we reach the shore and I enter my present life, a life that takes a deeper hold on me with each passing day.

From the landing I go to the library, or to the evening class that I am taking in Fiction Writing. On weekends I meet friends at a cafe or a nightclub.

Working on my assignments, I think sometimes of her drawings. Simple though they seemed, I am sure that she put a lot of effort into them. I picture her sitting in front of an empty sheet of paper for a long time, then rapidly drawing a few lines, then sitting back and contemplating them. Some pages she would just have to throw away, others she would keep. There is no going back, once pen touches paper.

I feel at home here, in my uncle's basement. He's a jolly, old man who does not find it odd that I am trying to be a writer.

Zindagi Itefaq Hai
(Life is Chance)

A gust came in through the window of Vishwanath Iyer's office at *The Daily Disquieter* and playfully blew a stack of paper off his untidy desk. Most of the sheets landed on the dusty floor, but one piece continued to float in the air. It was claimed by another gust, intent on more mischief, which blew the sheet out of the window. The page was enjoying its flight – oh, the lightness of being – when gravity staked its claim, and it fell, not straight like a stone, but rather, meandering like a temperamental kite, towards the *gulli,* the little lane two stories below. Vishwanath – Vish to colleagues and friends – was not a senior enough journalist to have an air conditioned office, or even a paperweight, any of which might have prevented the page from escaping.

Minutes later Vish entered his cubicle, nearly stepping on a typewritten sheet lying on the floor. Picture him with curly, unruly hair, glasses poised at the end of a long nose, wearing a sweaty, blue shirt. *The Disquieter*'s cartoonist would have enjoyed sketching him in this pose – one foot stuck in air, inches from the floor, chest rigid, mouth agape, hands petrified.

"Oh god!" said Vish and stooped to pick up the scattered sheets. His fingers seemed to lose the ability to firmly grasp objects that humans acquire very early in life and baboons even earlier. But after some effort, Vish had the pages in his grip. There was one missing! Now there was a gaping hole in the article that was to go as the second lead on the front page. And there was no copy.

Vish looked around wildly. He searched among the papers on his desk; he dove under it. He opened drawers and checked – just in case. Then he repeated his actions. It was no good. Page two had disappeared. Vish looked out of the window. Directly below, in the dingy little *gulli*, was a rubbish dump, with a cow nosing through it.

He rushed out of the room, in a foul mood. He had just received an earful from the publisher Jagdish Kukreja. And now this.

The day before, Vish had written a story in the honourable tradition of investigative journalism – a report about a land grab scam indicting the city's big builder, Ramkumar Singha. Singha's company routinely advertised their suburban housing complexes in *The Daily Disquieter*. Singha was also distantly related to Kukreja, being the second cousin of Kukreja's brother-in-law's aunt's husband. Singha had called Kukreja's secretary that morning, threatening to withdraw all advertising and sue *The Disquieter* for libel.

Vish had been egged on to do the exposé by *The Disquieter*'s flamboyant editor, Vikram Minuwalla. The story had taken up most of the tabloid's front page, the other eye catcher being a sexy condom ad. Kukreja never confronted Minuwalla, who would have resigned at the slightest reprimand. Instead, he directed his ire at underlings – reporters, sub-editors, typists, typesetters.

Minuwalla, with a reputation for brilliance and eccentricity, was a sought after editor. This was the first time he had condescended to work for an afternoon paper, his forte being national dailies, temples to good taste and worldly intelligence, or so they believed. Kukreja's business interests spanned telecommunications, chemicals and finance, yet Minuwalla made him uncomfortable. It was difficult to guess what went on in Minuwalla's busy brain from hour to hour, let alone say anything definitive about his motives in general.

Vish was Minuwalla's favourite reporter. This particularly singled him out for Kukreja's target practice. Half-an-hour earlier, on that fateful day, Vish had been typing out a story about a complicated and controversial amendment to Maharashtra State's Industrial Disputes Act. The amendment had been passed by the state's Lower House the day before. He was in the thick of it when a peon had come in saying that Kukreja wanted to see him at once. Turning away reluctantly from his story, Vish went over to Kukreja's posh office on the third floor of *The Disquieter* building.

"Why, why wasn't I consulted before the story was printed?" Kukreja thundered as soon as Vish stepped in through the door. At nearly six feet, the corpulent man cut an impressive figure, as he stood behind his desk, glaring at Vish.

The editorial department could have, at the very least, displayed some common sense and hinted at the builder's name, instead of being so brazenly direct about it. Did *they* want to shut the paper down? Did *they* want him to go bankrupt? Was that *their* ultimate goal? There was no teamwork in this organization, none whatsoever. The editorial department always did what *they* wanted without consulting the other departments. Kukreja ranted on and on.

Vish heard Kukreja out. This was clearly not the time to invoke the Indian Constitution, speak of the freedom of expression, elaborate on the right and proper role of a free press in a democracy, or point out that an editor's role was quite distinct from a publisher's. To argue that it was not very likely that Singha would sue because, for one thing, he did not have much of a case. *They* had covered *their* ass very well. That Singha would, in all likelihood, continue to advertise in *The Disquieter*, because he and Kukreja had other business dealings, which he would not want to jeopardize. That the paper's circulation had risen, and kept rising, since Minuwalla had taken over. There was no point saying anything, because he was merely a conduit. Later that day Vish would have to report everything to Minuwalla. Minuwalla's lips would curl up ever so slightly, and his eyes exhibit a tiny sparkle, from behind heavy glasses. Nothing brought Minuwalla greater happiness than a pissed-off publisher.

Kukreja cursed Minuwalla yet again as Vish left the room. He should have stayed with *The Disquieter*'s former *avatar* – cheesy centre spreads, Bollywood gossip, lots of sports news and the odd story about the municipal government bungling something or the other – *The Disquieter* did not receive much government advertising; that went to the morning papers. Could he afford the respectability that Minuwalla had brought to the paper? Could he afford investigative journalism, all the rage in the country, a fire that threatened to burn the moral fabric of the nation to cinders?

Vish's thoughts ran parallel as he hastened down the stairs. At one time he had believed that he would stake his life on investigative journalism, that upright pole which would eventually unfurl the flag of his triumphant success. Now all he could think about was how tired he felt. Eight months at the paper, strung like an unhappy Chinese lantern between Kukreja and Minuwalla, had worn him out. His mother, who had visited two months before from Bangalore, had remarked on his thinness, his careworn appearance, and suggested arranged marriage – the cure for all ills.

The cow regarded Vish balefully as he approached the rubbish dump.

"Shoo," he said to her urgently. "Go away."

The cow stared with large, deep eyes and swished her tail; she did not budge. Bloody cows, thought Vish. Animals with an IQ lower than dogs should be banished beyond the city gates. He struck some threatening poses before the impassive animal.

Hearing a sound from behind, Vish turned to find a skinny street child, dressed in stained, oversized half-pants, impressively bald. Vish pulled out his wallet and extracted a one rupee note from it. *"Isko bhagao,"* he told the urchin, waving the money. *Get rid of her.*

The urchin leapt forward at once and pushed the cow, shouting insults at her. The cow took the hint and ambled down the alley, loudly registering her protest. Vishwanath burrowed into the stinking garbage which contained large quantities of soiled paper in many colours, textures, sizes; mostly discarded press releases. The urchin tugged at his sleeve.

"Good boy," said Vish, giving him the note. Then he continued his search. The boy joined in, flinging handfuls of garbage here and there. Vish heard heavy footsteps and looked up, to find himself nose to nose with a policeman.

"*Kya horelai yaha*?" the cop demanded. *What's going on here?*

Vish felt repulsed; Bombay Hindi was so uncouth. Vish, though a Southie, had grown up in the North. He had been taught Hindi by a teacher who wrote beautiful Urdu poetry. Bombay was a slaughter house for Hindi and Urdu − oh those mellifluous tongues which he had come to adore during his painfully romantic adolescence!

Suddenly Vish noticed that there was garbage all over the place. Before he could explain the situation, the urchin told the policeman in a shrill, convincing voice that he had been paid to search through the garbage and showed him the rupee Vish had given him.

Vish could not believe his ears. As an investigative journalist, he encountered human folly and treachery at every turn, but that had not turned him into a cynic. If anything, it had made him more sentimental.

Minutes later, he returned to the editorial department empty handed. The urchin had taken to his heels, laughing, and the cop had accepted the fact that Vish was the injured party. Vish and the cop had kicked the garbage back in place, becoming almost friends in the process. It occurred to Vish that, though it was apparently illegal to have rubbish spread around, it seemed okay to have it pile up for days at one spot. He had held his peace. The *paan*-chewing policeman may not have had a high tolerance for Aristotelian logic.

"Want to take a look at Rajni's report?" Arun, one of the sub-editors, called out to him as he walked into the editorial section. Rajni, the pretty new trainee reporter, had made an impression on Vish since she had joined the organization two months before.

Unfortunately, there was no way of calculating if the opposite was also true.

They had started out sharing insights on Italo Calvino's fiction and progressed very well from that point, conversationally, that is. During the past few weeks, Rajni had started consulting him about the articles she wrote, surely a healthy sign. But Rajni also had tête-à-têtes with Royce, the crime reporter, a brash young man who wore loud shirts, was an expert jiver and sped around town on a heavy-duty mo-bike. Rajni seemed to have quite an appetite for violent crime. How could someone who enjoyed Pablo Neruda's poetry smack her lips at the latest gang killing, Vish often wondered.

"No time," Vish muttered. He did not want to think about anyone else's report but focus instead on his own, one-legged story.

★ ★ ★

Abbas took a short cut through *The Disquieter gul-li*, passing underneath Vish's window at the precise moment that page two made its descent. He felt it brush against his hair and reached for it instinctively. Absorbed in the cricket commentary pouring out from the small transistor radio clutched to his ear, he did not bother to look at his find. It must be an ad of some sort, he thought, shoving the paper into the *khadi* bag that hung from his shoulder. He would attend to it later. The India-Australia test match was at a crucial point and the ears of the nation were firmly turned Down Under.

★ ★ ★

Back in his cubicle, Vish surveyed the dingy space. Paint was perpetually peeling off the walls, dirt clung obstinately to corners, cobwebs sprang up overnight despite the hostility they inspired in the cleaning woman. What was he doing here anyway?

The most important part of the article was gone. Page Two contained a lengthy quote on the Industrial Disputes Act amendment from Mayank Bakshi, a High Court judge. All he had to do was call Justice Bakshi and get the quote again. It wasn't such a big deal. Vish picked up the phone and asked the operator to get him the Justice.

"But you just spoke to him in the morning, no?" the operator protested.

"Be a sweetheart and get me his number again, Nilu," said Vish with all the sweetness he could muster. "It's a matter of life and death."

"Isn't it always?" said Nilu, going off the line.

Vish lit a cigarette while he waited. The nicotine coursed happily through his bloodstream, joining other excited chemicals there. The merry toxins decided to start a Heavy Metal band and set up a practice session on the spot. Vish continued smoking purposefully, feeling much better. He had tried to cut down after he had overheard Rajni telling a colleague that she hated men smoking, but loved the smell of whisky on their breath. And if it were premium scotch, all the better.

Arun stepped into the cubicle just as Vish was stubbing out his cigarette. He had grown up in the North, in Lucknow, the fabled city of kings, writers, connoisseurs, and was Vish's friend and confidante. Arun made impatient noises on hearing the news about Page Two.

"I can't understand why you people don't make a copy," he said. "Don't you have carbon paper?"

Vish said nothing.

"You know you're supposed to make two copies," Arun persisted. Then he assumed a more sympathetic tone, "Don't you have notes?"

Vish explained that he had been typing the first draft of the piece when Nilu had got him the High Court judge on the phone. Vish had written down the lengthy quote, full of legalese that he could barely comprehend, at the back of Page Two. He had been planning to retype the whole story with the quote in the right place when Kukreja had sent for him.

"Don't worry, you'll get the quote," said Arun, sliding off the desk on which he was perched. "Don't forget we are going out for lunch for Meenakshi's birthday."

He departed in a good mood. This was the first disaster of the day. There would be others as the sun climbed higher in the sky. As a sub editor, Arun was denied direct participation in the hurly burly of public life, and forced to get his kicks from internal fuck-ups.

Arun's a good chap, Vish mused, wishing that he was a sub-editor. All Arun had to do was sit and sub copy, while he, Vish, was expected to perform tricks all the time. It was hard to follow one acrobatic turn with another that was higher, faster, better. True there were underhand deals all over the place, waiting to be exposed, but why did people have such an appetite for reading about them?

The phone rang shrilly, scaring him. "Justice Bakshi's office, Sir," said Nilu in her best secretarial school voice. Vish asked for the Justice and was told that he was not available. He had come in early, for a mere two hours, and had left the city, soon after.

"What do you mean?" said Vish.

"He's gone to attend his granddaughter's wedding in Delhi," chirped Bakshi's secretary. "I myself booked the ticket. AC Second Class."

"I don't believe this," Vish muttered, half to himself.

"Do you know that his granddaughter is getting married to the son of the Maharaja of Ujjain who is a MLA who ..."

"Never mind," Vish said, cutting her short. He asked for details about the train and, for the second time that day, bounded downstairs at a dangerous speed, barely remembering to grab his note pad. He decided not to bother with a taxi, wishing he had invested in a two-wheeler. Not a mo-bike, but a scooter would have been all right.

He walked rapidly towards Victoria Terminus. The train might be late. There had been a big derailment just the day before, unfortunately not on the route to Delhi, but in the Southern state of Tamil Nadu. The morning papers — those high and mighty national dailies who thought they were the cat's whiskers — had gone to town on the accident, paying scant attention to the Industrial Disputes Act amendment. They would front page the story tomorrow, the bloody vultures, always sniffing for fresh blood spills. Vish just had to get his story in that day.

The station was a tide of bodies, a cacophony of sounds — human and mechanical, a solid flow of heat-resistant energy. Nevertheless, the announcer's steady voice, talking alternatively in Marathi, Hindi and English, managed to prevail over the chaos. Vish impatiently scanned the electronic display board. The Bombay-Delhi Express was not mentioned. He turned towards a *coolie* who was hurrying past and inquired about the train.

"Just now only it has gone," said a shrivelled-up, old man who had overheard him.

Vish turned away. Fuck. Oh fuck. A wave of fatigue hit him, making him somewhat dizzy. Then it passed. It must be his low blood pressure. He wove his way slowly through the crowd, letting himself be pushed around, wishing he was on the train, Delhi-bound, back at St. Stephan's College, doing his Bachelors in History. He could have gone on to do his M.A. and become a lecturer. After all, he had got a First Class First. The Head of the Department had called him to his office and said he should study further and that he was eligible for a scholarship. Or he could have gone abroad, to the States, where so many of his classmates had ended up. But he had chosen journalism because his grandfather, a freedom fighter, had wanted him to be a newspaperman, and had brainwashed him since childhood.

"Journalists will be the revolutionaries of independent India," he had said. Or words to that effect. So here he was. The wrong man for the job. The wronged man as well.

What was the next stop for the train? Kalyan. The train would take about 45 minutes to get there. The only way to intercept was to grow wings and fly. Kukreja owned a private plane. A faint smile played on Vish's lips for the first time that day. It was crazy to entertain the idea that Kukreja, who had bawled him out, would sanction a flight in his plane, his most cherished possession. He was more likely to give him the sack. The only thing that stood between Kukreja and his walking papers was Minuwalla. And God only knew how long the restless Minuwalla would stay at *The Disquieter.* There was no Justice in the world. That was obvious. None whatsoever.

Back at the office, Ganpat came around on his second round and placed a glass of boiled-to-death, brown liquid that passed for tea, on the window sill.

Vishwanath fumbled in his pockets for change, but couldn't find any.

"*Baad mein dena,*" said Ganpat, carrying on, the tea tray gracefully balanced with one hand over his right shoulder, his face as peaceful as the Buddha's. *Give it later.* His demeanour did nothing to calm Vish, who downed the cup at one go and lit a cigarette.

Could he find a replacement for the dear, departed Justice? He had to make the story work somehow. Could he interview someone else? Not really, because Justice Bakshi was the country's foremost authority on labour law. He had written weighty tomes on the subject that would have given most people acute constipation. He had also set scintillating precedents as a High Court judge. There was another lawyer in Delhi, Bakshi's former assistant, who might be able to help. But would he say anything, given the controversial nature of the amendment?

Arun came in to collect money. They were going to buy a gift for Meenakshi, the birthday girl. Vish gave him a ten-rupee note.

Vish asked Nilu to get him Chandrakant Bhatt, the Delhi lawyer. As he waited, the train of thought that had started at VT station resumed its journey. Yes, Delhi. Had he chosen to live there, chaste Hindi would have surrounded him like the morning mist that graced the city in winter. He could have attended *mushairyas*, listening to renowned Urdu poets through enchanted nights. This job did not allow him to plan anything in advance. In any case, he was too tired during his time off to do anything but sleep. Investigative journalism was all about pinning down the truth, whatever the hell that was. That's what Minuwalla believed. He did not have the stomach for investigative journalism nor The Truth, Vish decided.

The phone rang again. Nilu had got him Bhatt's office, but Bhatt was out of town. He was in Amritsar. Doing what? Vish asked in exasperation. Attending an important meeting, replied the secretary mechanically. Vish hung up, fearing for the justice system, what with judges and lawyers prancing all over the country instead of staying put, applying themselves seriously to their work.

Vish stared moodily out of the window. There was not much to look at save the grimy façade of an old building. He turned purposefully to his typewriter, put in a sheet of paper and started typing out his story – flat, almost pointless without the all-important quote. Then he handed the copy to Arun.

"Don't give me a byline," he said.

"Get a drink, *yaar*," Arun said sympathetically.

"I don't think I'll come for lunch," Vish said. Rajni would be there. And Royce. There was no way he could compete with the eternally buoyant Royce today.

Vish made his way slowly to the *Rubaiyat of Omar Khayyam*, a seedy, dimly-lit, backstreet restaurant, popular with serious drinkers and randy lovers, because the waiters turned a blind eye on petting couples and clients who methodically drank themselves into a stupor. It was the nearest watering hole for the *Disquieter* crowd.

En route was another garbage heap, a prince of garbage heaps if not the queen or king. Vish felt himself being pulled magnetically to its periphery. A stink rose from the pile of plastic, paper, leftover food, discarded items. Rubbish. Rubbish. Rubbish. A piece of yellowish paper caught his eye. It was backside up and obviously typewritten. He pulled it out carefully from under a coconut shell. It wasn't Page Two. A young rag-picker with a grubby face and dreadlocks eyed Vish curiously as he turned dispiritedly away.

Vish found a corner table at the restaurant. Nursing a peg of cheap, local whisky – alas, no scotch for an underpaid reporter; munching moodily on *masala chana* – the snack was on the house – Vish contemplated the crude mural of a turbaned, bearded man in a long, white *kurta* – presumably the legendary poet, Omar Khayyam – reclining on the ground, languidly holding out a wine glass, while a half-veiled woman in harem pants and a bikini top coyly poured him a drink from a pitcher. The touching tableau was set against the backdrop of a mini waterfall and two spindly-looking trees. The artist had put in his masterstroke at the recumbent man's feet – a loaf of bread and a crudely-drawn, open book. He had painted his name, D.D. Pujari, with a flourish, at the bottom right.

For an absurd but delightful second, Vish imagined he was Omar Khayyam and Rajni the provocative beauty. On a normal day he would have spent some time embroidering the fantasy, but not today. He took a large gulp of the whisky and let out a deep sigh as a mournful Hindi film song started up suddenly from a nearby loudspeaker.

★ ★ ★

Farha was waiting for Abbas at their usual table, sipping *limbu pani*, reading *Femina*. No sooner had Abbas sat down, Farha took hold of his bag and started rummaging through it, as was her habit. Being the possessive type, she staked her absolute claim on Abbas and everything he owned. She discovered Page

Two almost immediately and started grilling Abbas: Where had he found it? What was it?

Abbas was in no mood for an interrogation. He had had a busy day. He had got up at 5:30 am to attend his morning law classes. Then he had gone to his brother-in-law's import-export firm, where he worked part-time. After their early lunch, he would go back to his brother-in-law's office, and then, in the evening, he would make the rounds delivering wedding cards that his sister designed and printed, as a small business.

But Farha persisted: "Take a look at it, Abbas. It looks interesting."

Abbas took hold of Page Two just as the waiter came to take their orders. He ordered the chicken *kebab* plate, Farha the mutton.

Abbas crooked his eyebrow. "How come you're eating mutton today?"

"Just like that. For a change."

"Tomorrow you'll show up with a new boyfriend and say the same thing."

"Read the paper, sweetheart."

Abbas glanced at the typewritten words. Weird. He looked at Farha and shrugged.

"Read the other side," said Farha. Abbas turned the page. Suddenly he looked animated. "Hey! It says Justice Bakshi ... and there's something about the Industrial Disputes Act ..."

"What?"

"Let me read it ... okay? Remember I told you about Justice Bakshi who came to college as a guest lecturer?"

"Yes. You said he was an impressive speaker."

The *kebabs* arrived, but Abbas ignored his favourite dish to re-read Page Two while Farha tucked appreciatively into her aromatic meal.

"My guess is that this is part of an article of some sort about the Industrial Disputes Act amendment," he said after a minute.

"Is it important?"

"Yeah. I mean … I don't know. I haven't seen anything about the amendment in the papers. But it just went through."

"Where did you get this?"

"No idea."

"Think Abbas, think."

Abbas started eating. He reflected over his morning and recalled the dingy *gulli*, the rubbish heap, the paper falling out of the sky. He described the location to Farah.

Farha had been to *The Disquieter* office a couple of times to visit her friend Priya, who worked in the ad department. Feeling very pleased with her detective work, she surmised that the page had come from *The Disquieter* building.

"Do you think this is lost property? Should we return it?" she asked anxiously.

"Lost? No, I don't think so. Anyway, there's no way I would ever help that paper, that bloody rag."

Farha looked questioning.

"Don't you remember how they accused my uncle of being involved with that smuggler? Kaneeza aunty fell ill after that."

"But that was because of your uncle's *lafda* with his secretary, no?" Farha said.

Abbas ignored her and concentrated on his food, fuming. What a silly girl she was. Really!

"Well newspapers, you know how they are. They like to create controversy," Farha said, trying to make up.

She ordered a pista *kulfi*. As they spooned through it together, they were friends again. Abbas complained that he was feeling cold and implored Farha to come and sit on his lap. Farha obliged, giggling.

★ ★ ★

Seeing a chance of escape, Page Two slipped off the seat and fell inches from Vish's feet. Vish, sitting at the next table, had been eavesdropping on the conversation, his desperation reaching heart-attack levels. Now he bent down, ever so swift and stealthy, and picked up the page. Alas, Page Two was not fated to be free for long.

Leaving some money on the table, Vish tiptoed out of the restaurant, observed only by a drunk drooling into his drink. The smooching couple of course had no eyes for him.

Outside, he broke into an exhilarating run. He would just be able to get his story in before *The Disquieter* went to press.

Freire Stopped in Bombay

Dilip stood hungry and listless, on the tiny balcony of his fourth floor hostel room, looking down at the busy street.

It was Saturday afternoon, half day for schools and most offices. The primary school across the street had just discharged its load. Some of the children were already being led home by their maidservants or mothers. They dragged their feet, looking longingly at the pavement vendors selling sweets, ice cream, peanuts and spicy snacks, balloons, whistles, tops and other small toys. Their guardians kept a firm hold on them, urging them to hurry. They were distracted as well by the cars approaching to pick up other children.

The scene was noisy as well as busy. Cars reversed with a grating sound, horns blared, brakes slammed, doors banged, radios played. Every so often a motorcycle roared down the street, weaving dangerously through the traffic. Sometimes one would stop in front of the hostel, and a young man or a couple got off and entered the building.

Three young men in jeans, t-shirts and dark glasses loitered outside the hostel gate, smoking. They leered at every woman who walked by, whistling, commenting and laughing. Louts, Dilip thought.

They gave the hostel a bad reputation. Idiots! His expression turned approving as a soberly dressed office worker, carrying a briefcase, passed by. Probably he had just finished lunch and was going back to work. One of the unfortunates who did not have a half-day, but at least his stomach was full.

Dilip experienced a rush of saliva as he pictured lunch. They must have begun serving the mid-day meal at the hostel canteen. But there was no way he could eat there; he had cancelled the meal plan months ago because his scholarship instalments were so erratic.

Trrrrrring – a little boy let his bicycle bell go, as he pedalled jauntily down the street. He reminded Dilip of his sisters and cousins in Wadgav, the little village where he had grown up. These kids in Bombay were middle-class, neatly moulded into their school uniforms, while his siblings attended school in well-worn, patched clothes. But like these children, his siblings too were growing up fast. At 18, his sister Malti was a woman. She had completed her matriculation and was already engaged. She would be married in two months! He had a hard time adjusting to that reality.

Malti was a strong and serene presence in Dilip's life. She was only two years younger than him, and they had a lot in common. After her marriage, she was going to move out of Wadgav and study nursing. Her fiancé, Pradeep, was a lucky guy. He worked as a clerk with a state government department in Bombay. A family friend had brought about the match.

Malti would move to Bombay soon. This had been a constant reassurance to Dilip, but now he felt that it didn't matter. Nothing would change; Malti's arrival would not make the slightest difference to his situation. He was doomed, well and truly doomed.

Looking at the receding figure of the boy on the bike, Dilip wished that he had his battered old bicycle with him, here in Bombay. There was a time when he had cycled 20 km every day, sometimes in pouring rain, balancing an umbrella in one hand, managing to steer his bike with the other. He had to somehow make it to his secondary school in the nearest town, even during the monsoons. Wadgav didn't have a *pukka* road then, and the dusty path would turn to sludge after a few downpours. They would sink large, flat stones into the mud and he would step carefully over them, carrying his bike, trying to keep his old school uniform clean. His mother took pride in washing and ironing it, by putting it flat under a mattress. The government had eventually built a *pukka* road. By then, Dilip was on his way. He had won a state government scholarship to do his B.A. in Bombay.

He rarely thought about Wadgav. In fact, he deliberately avoided thinking about it. Yet thoughts from the past had a way of sneaking into his head, dropping in like unwelcome relatives, demanding tea, snacks and gossip. He hadn't written home for nearly two months. He had two letters from Malti and one from his father lying in the top drawer of his study table, unopened. Pradeep had come to see him a couple of weeks ago. Malti must have asked him to pay a visit. Dilip had told the peon to tell him that he was not in his room.

He glanced at the cheque for 500 rupees in his hand. It had arrived yesterday afternoon, too late to make a bank deposit, though a mere ten days late this time. He could make a deposit only on Monday, and withdraw some money. He had one rupee in his pocket. No, that was one rupee, 10 paisa.

Wada-pav! The bread soft and warm, brown and shiny on top, white and slightly dusty on the side, with a thin coating of red-hot chili chutney inside, and the all-important *wadas*: melt-in-the-mouth mashed potato balls dipped in a chick-pea batter and fried to perfection. The memory of garlic tantalized his tongue and he felt his gut contract.

Matherchoth! *Motherfucker*! He had the urge to spit out the word so it would land with a thud on the street, form a venomous stream, and flow, flow like an open sewer through the city. People would see it coming and jump out of the way. The sewer would run to Bombay University's Revenue Department, stopping at the feet of one Mr. Mahajan, Chief Accountant, who signed all the cheques. Mr. Mahajan, looking down from his desk would be terrified, and find himself choking on the stench …

Dilip wanted to crush the cheque in his fist and toss it into the Arabian sea, which wasn't very far. If Dilip had pushed himself out over the balcony railing and craned his neck to the left, something he had done just last week, he would have caught a glimpse of blue through the fronds of a palm tree. Marine Drive ran more or less perpendicular to the street where the hostel stood. If he licked his lips he could taste salt on them.

The sea had fascinated Dilip when he first got here, two years ago, coming as he did from interior Maharashtra, which was arid and rugged. He used to go for long walks along the breezy promenade that was Marine Drive, alone, or with his hostel buddies. The sunsets were spectacular, particularly during the monsoons when the sea neighed like a high-spirited mare and waves crashed against the rocks, sending jets of water into the air, under a flaming sky – gold, orange and pink.

At night the sky would turn clear and dark, but the sea would be darker still, a bit restless, foaming at the mouth, mysterious and inviting. A balmy breeze, sweet enough to soothe the most troubled brow, would blow ashore, wiping away every trace of the day's plentiful sweat. The lights from the high-rise buildings that dotted the Drive would gleam incredibly, magically bright – the Queen's Necklace.

Vishnu, Dilip's *jigari dost*, his *best buddy*, did not care for the name Queen's Necklace. Those bloody Brits with their la-di-da ways, he would say. "We Indians are such assholes. We just carry on with their fucking, colonial shit."

Dilip's classmates would start laughingly debating the point, half-heartedly defending the good things about British Rule – schools, hospitals, railways, the parliamentary system. And cricket. People would be pro or against, depending on their mood. Vishnu would continue in a staunchly nationalistic spirit, sometimes quoting the leaders of the Independence Movement. The uncompromising Subhash Chandra Bose was his favourite.

Dilip would listen to these conversations, fascinated. He admired the way Vishnu freely abused the British, or for that matter anyone and anything. Ramesh, who liked to play the devil's advocate, would make and stick to the counter argument, trying to outshout his opponents and wear them down. But you could not beat Vishnu for sheer stubbornness. Dilip enjoyed these battles of will and wit. India would have been a much more peaceful country if people stayed with heated debates, without picking up stones, he thought.

Months passed before he started contributing to the discussions. It was not just his shyness that held him back; it was also his English.

Dilip's father had made it a point to send him to a good secondary school which, though Marathi-medium, was known for teaching English well. Yes it was a long way from home, but what was the alternative, Dilip's father said, if a neighbour or relative dared to question his choice. The school that was nearer home just would not do.

Mrs. Sitara, Dilip's English teacher, took a special interest in him. She let him take four books out of the library at a time, though the official limit was two. Dilip had usually chosen two books in English and two in Marathi, his mother tongue. Mrs. Sitara also frequently picked him to read aloud in the English period.

Dilip's cousin, Milind, a teacher in Nagpur, had encouraged Dilip's father to subscribe to an English newspaper on the weekends. "What a luxury – a newspaper, that too in English!" Dilip's mother would say from time to time. No one else read the paper though Dilip's father glanced through it sometimes. Dilip's mother, who did not speak English and held it in uneasy contempt, never failed to bring up this extravagance whenever she and her husband had a quarrel over money.

Milind, who was the only other family member fluent in English, encouraged Dilip to listen to the BBC, giving him a transistor radio on his 12th birthday. Dilip's English and his general knowledge were very good; his father was proud of him for that.

Still, it was a very different sort of English that they spoke here, in Bombay. Vishnu's English was much like his, strongly accented with Marathi. Most of their classmates had gone to English-medium schools; naturally they had a better accent. And some had gone to Convents, giving them the best accent. At first Dilip had been acutely aware that, though he was fluent, his accent was all wrong. And he lacked some of the vocabulary his classmates had. He had consciously worked to blunt his accent. The new words he had picked up easily enough. Vishnu, he observed, was not encumbered by his accent. He spoke as freely and confidently as their better-off colleagues.

After a while Dilip's accent had not mattered much. He had brains and he was better informed than his peers. More hard-working too. If the first thing his friends looked for was how "cool" you were, the second was intelligence. Dilip did not have an uncle in the U.S. to send him Levi jeans or a Sony walkman, nor did he have a Jimi Hendrix record collection, but he could hold forth on a range of subjects. He had found himself becoming voluble as the months passed, the casual camaraderie of his friends cushioning his self-confidence. He was at ease with the English-medium crowd as well as the vernacular medium students. He was not a part of either clique, but to some extent he belonged to both.

Dilip rarely went for walks on Marine Drive now. Their gang had gradually dispersed, some of their classmates moving in with relatives or finding paying guest accommodation. These days Dilip passed the time sitting in his room, staring at the walls. Sometimes he would turn on the radio, but it only provided some background sound. He didn't really listen to any of the programs.

Time had changed its quality and the days had somehow shrunk. Maybe because it took him longer to do things. Maybe because he slept so erratically. He hardly went to lectures these days and, when he did, he couldn't concentrate. Even the brilliant sociology teacher, Professor Wagle, did not hold Dilip's attention anymore. You had to pay attention to take good notes. Now he depended on Vishnu for notes.

And he hadn't even bothered with those for the past couple of weeks.

Not so long ago it was Dilip who had the most up-to-date and detailed notes, taken in his beautiful, angular hand. His friends would borrow his notes from him every time they bunked a lecture to go to a movie, romance a girl or to just sit around talking, in the college canteen.

Dilip turned away from the street and entered his room. He dropped the cheque on his desk, where it fell to its rest, among half-written sheets of paper and open textbooks. Lying down on the narrow, iron bed with its sweaty bedcover, Dilip turned his gaze towards the wall.

He was hungry; in fact, he was starving. All he had eaten the day before was an egg curry-rice for lunch. Vishnu had tried to buy him breakfast in the morning, but he had refused, pretending that he had more than the wretched rupee in his pocket. The meal-a-day routine that he had been on for a week, or longer, left him cranky and disoriented. It seemed to upset his stomach. He would wake up at odd hours during the night with cramps and he felt light-headed when he got out of bed in the morning.

Vishnu had invited him to go with him to his cousin's house in Dahisar for the weekend. But Dilip had made up an excuse. He didn't want to see people. People always asked questions about his family, his studies, his future plans. They wanted to talk all the time – about politics, TV, sports, and the sorry state of the country. It exhausted and irritated him.

Besides that, going to Dahisar involved a long train journey, and he had never got used to the local trains in Bombay. Luckily his college was walking distance from his hostel. The crowds, the stench, the incredible crush of closely packed bodies on the local trains made Dilip anxious. He dreaded having to force his way into a second-class men's compartment. He had even experienced groping hands once or twice and felt really sick. How could people be so disgusting?

Vishnu didn't seem to mind commuting. But then he was a Bombay boy – *bindaas*, totally cool. He had been born there, and lived in the hostel only because his parents had moved back to Deolali, their native town.

In any case, Dilip had no money for the train fare. Vishnu had offered to pay, but how could he let him? As it is Vishnu, who was quite hard up, spent so much money on him.

Dilip wondered sometimes how much of the fierce affection and protectiveness that Vishnu displayed towards him was personal; and how much linked to the fact that they were both Dalit.

Vishnu felt much more strongly about being Dalit than Dilip did. Though named after a very important god in the Hindu holy trinity, Vishnu was a neo-Buddhist, unlike Dilip, who considered himself Hindu. Dilip's mother had an altar at home that housed several Hindu deities. She worshipped them all every day. She fasted and observed various Hindu festivals throughout the year. At the same time, a faded, black and white photograph of Babasaheb Ambedkar, the great Dalit leader who had urged Dalits to turn Buddhist, occupied a prominent place on the veranda wall. A garland of bright pink plastic flowers framed it – a mark of respect. His mother made it a point to dust the photograph regularly.

Vishnu was more conscious about being Dalit because his uncle was involved in Dalit politics. Vishnu had heard Dalit leaders speak; he had gone on protest marches and rallies, though his activism had tapered off after he entered university. He had lent Babasaheb

Ambedkar's biography to Dilip. Ambedkar had studied at Elphinstone College, where Dilip and Vishnu were now studying, a fact that Vishnu referred to with pride from time to time.

Dilip, growing up in a village with a mostly Dalit population, among small farmers, farm labourers and workers who sought seasonal employment in cities, with just two upper-caste families who were not that much better off than the others, felt he did not share Vishnu's passion about the injustice done to low-caste people. Perhaps he should. Perhaps he should be angry. Anger that was chili-hot like the *wada-pav* chutney and inflamed the tongue and the senses.

All he felt was tired, and hungry. He would skip dinner as well and get something to eat tomorrow. His stomach rumbled but he paid no heed; he was used to ignoring its protests. He knew the pattern now – intense hunger pangs followed by a numbness. Then a calm would descend on him and he would fall asleep.

Next to Dilip's pillow lay a well-thumbed copy of *Pedagogy of the Oppressed*. Dilip picked up the book and allowed it to fall open. Page 125. He read randomly: "On the other hand, it would be a false premise to believe that activism (which is not true action) is the road to revolution. Men will be truly critical if they live the plentitude of the praxis, that is, if their action encompasses a critical reflection which increasingly organizes their thinking ..."

Dilip let *Pedagogy* fall from his hands. The words he had just read made no sense, even though he knew the book intimately, having read it from cover to cover half a dozen times. His one desire had been to possess a new copy, since the one he had was dog-eared.

Dilip owned few books. He was used to getting them out of libraries or occasionally borrowing them from friends. What was the use of buying books, his mother used to say. A library was where a book belonged, not a home. He had never particularly wanted to own a book, but that was before he became obsessed with *Pedagogy of the Oppressed*.

He had found the book at a used bookstore in Walkeshwar, for two rupees. Prof. Wagle had spoken with great enthusiasm about the book, and mentioned its author, Paulo Freire, in one of his first lectures that term. Freire the liberator! Freire the intellectual! Freire the educator! Freire the humanist par excellence!

Dilip had gone to the Professor's Common Room after that lecture. A peon, loitering at the door, had told Dilip that he would summon Professor Wagle, casting him a look that said: "Keep Out." Seconds later, Prof. Wagle bounced towards Dilip.

"Come in, come in. You wanted to see me, no?"

Dilip nodded and followed the Prof. into the high-ceiling room with a long table surrounded by many chairs. Against the wall were antique benches, a grandfather clock, which was not working, and heavy, book-lined cupboards. Perched on top of the cupboards were dusty shields and cups, won by the college for participating in various sports and cultural events. Dilip felt as if he was breathing the rarified air of scholarship and intellectual enquiry. Who in Wadgav would have ever imagined that he, Dilip Bodhare, would be inside the Professor's Common Room of the prestigious Elphinstone College one day?

Prof. Wagle took him to a bench and said: "Have a seat." Sitting next to him, he asked Dilip some routine questions about his studies, ending with: "Everything okay?"

"Yes Sir. But ... I ... Can I ask you a question about something that is outside the syllabus?"

"Of course, of course."

Dilip asked him about Freire. The Professor was obviously pleased with the inquiry. Freire was a famous Brazilian educator, he explained, not just an educator, but a revolutionary educator who had developed a unique method for teaching illiterates that had an impact all over the world. Freire wanted to encourage the development of a critical consciousness so that people examined the social structures that kept them in oppressive situations. *Pedagogy of the Oppressed*, which held the key to Freire's ideas, had been so controversial in Brazil that Freire had been forced to live in exile in the U.S.A. for many years.

"Brilliant!" Prof. Wagle said. "He is truly brilliant." Dilip found it hard to imagine the brilliance of a man so highly recommended by someone as learned as the Professor. The Prof. urged him to read *Pedagogy of the Oppressed.*

"Is Freire still alive?" Dilip wanted to know.

"He is alive and well, as far as I know. And he lives in Brazil now." This fact too had made an impression on Dilip. Most of the Great Men he had read, or read about, were dead.

"You are doing good work, Dilip," the Professor said. "The college is proud of you, and so, I am sure, are your people."

Dilip wondered what he meant by that. Did he mean his family or the Dalits, as a whole? Probably the latter.

"By the way," the Prof. said as Dilip turned to go, "did you know that Freire came to India in the 1970s?"

"Did he come to Bombay?"

"I am not sure of that. He probably did."

Dilip turned so that he lay facing the room with his back to the wall. Suddenly he was nostalgic for the narrow, low-lit, dusty lanes of Wadgav, the smell of things growing and decomposing, the coolness of the mud floor that his mother and sisters washed and smoothed down every day with cow dung; the smoky sweetness of the night air with wood fires burning everywhere, the family gathered together in the courtyard for the evening meal, the eggplant *bharta* so incredibly tasty, made from vegetables just-picked from his mother's little garden behind their brick house, his father smoking *bidis*, sometimes listening to the transistor, Dilip sitting with Malti after the meal, playing a game of cards by the light of a kerosene lamp because the electricity had gone off for the nth time that day, while their younger sisters constantly pestered them to let them join the game – brats as persistent as mosquitoes that had to be swatted away.

Dilip rolled onto his stomach. The *paan-walla* who operated outside the hostel in the evenings had his radio tuned to Vividh Bharati. Snatches of an old, Hindi film song wafted up his room via the balcony: "*Jhumka gira re, Bareli ke bazaar mein jhumka gira re ...*" *My earring fell at the market in Bareli* ... He could hear other sounds – conversation, laughter, television, ping pong – filtering in through the slightly open door.

When he woke up again, everything was quiet in the immediate vicinity. He could hear the muted sound of cars on Marine Drive and the faint, industrial hum of the city, which meant that it was after midnight. Sleep had swallowed his day like a python that swallows a rat whole. Many snakes curled around Dilip's life these days, poised to strike.

He got up a little unsteadily and went out into the balcony.

The street stood empty. There were no lights in any of the buildings, only the streetlights were on. He was wide awake and hungry. He wished he had a biscuit to nibble on. The image of a simple, glucose biscuit made his mouth water. His mother always gave him a packet for the bus ride from Wadgav to Bombay. They were just five hours, and worlds, apart. The mud and brick houses, the wells and hand pumps, the fields and farm animals gave way to cluttered, little towns with shops and houses close together, much postered movie-halls, rickshaws and cars, the luxury of streetlights. Then the hills, salt marshes and coconut trees of Bombay's suburbs loomed into view. The city was massive, overwhelming, layered, stinking of chemicals and car exhaust, intoxicating. A place where every turn could bring you upon something unexpected – an elephant, a hotel that rose up to the sky, 20-foot statues of Lord Ganesh, a girl in a miniskirt.

But Dilip's world was confined to the hostel, to the street. Even his college did not seem to belong to him any more. How long was it going to go on like this?

A month before he had gathered courage to call Mr. Mahajan at the Revenue Department. He was passed on from person to person while a line of people gathered to use the hostel phone. Finally, Mahajan had come on the line. No, there was nothing he could do to release the cheques sooner; he had to wait for them to be approved, to come in. What could he do? He was totally helpless. Write a letter of complaint if you like, he told Dilip in a tone that suggested that this would not improve matters. Dilip had decided not to bother.

He looked down at the street. It was quite far down. There had been a discussion among his college mates once about suicide – what was the best way? Jumping from the 3rd floor meant badly broken bones and perhaps death. Jumping from the 4th floor meant death, certain death. Dilip looked again at the concrete slabs, straight down — far, far away. Shivering a little, he came back in and sat down on his bed.

What would Freire have done in his situation? He had read about Freire's life in the introduction to *Pedagogy of the Oppressed*. It said that Freire's middle-class family had suffered a setback and Freire had experienced hunger too. What sort of hunger? How acute?

Freire had shared his hunger with his family. Dilip's hunger was all his own, claiming him in a desolate hostel room, in the mammoth city of Bombay, whose streets were paved with gold and rife with beggars.

After buying *Pedagogy of the Oppressed*, Dilip had read it non-stop, looking up difficult words in the dictionary he had won as a prize in Class 10, for standing first.

After a few reads he felt that he understood what Freire was saying. More or less. The ideas in the book were certainly far out. They were really something else! Like the student and the teacher being partners, engaging in a dialogue to learn together.

He agreed with everything Freire said about the relationship between the oppressor and oppressed. Freire explained so very clearly how the oppressor managed to fool the oppressed by making them believe in their inferiority, by convincing them that his beliefs were right, theirs wrong. And then throwing them scraps, making them applaud his charity!

Dilip had bumped into Prof. Wagle soon after his third reading of *Pedagogy of the Oppressed*, and had blurted out that he liked the book.

"I knew you would," the Professor said warmly. "I think you should do a presentation about it in class. There's no time this term, but we can fit it in next term. We will discuss the book first, you and I, then you can write an outline for your presentation."

Dilip agreed, feeling slightly anxious but excited. As he turned to go, Prof. Wagle called out to him.

"Freire did come to Bombay," he said, looking earnestly at Dilip through his thick glasses. At 60, the Prof. retained a boyish enthusiasm, and Dilip was bathed in its light. "After you asked me I dug around a bit. There's even a book written about a seminar he conducted here. But I can't find it. Probably out of print."

Dilip looked into Prof. Wagle's watery, old eyes, bright with delight, and smiled. Yes, that was something – Freire in Bombay. It made his ideas flesh and bone, and he suspected that Freire being here meant a lot to the Professor as well.

"Bye, Sir," he said gently. As he turned away he caught sight of a quick wave from the professor that bordered on a half salute.

So they were going to dialogue just as Freire had suggested! They were going to interact as equals – he and Prof. Wagle! Professor Wagle must think well of him. After that Dilip often day dreamed about their next meeting in the Professor's Common Room. He gave a lot of thought to the presentation, deciding that he would incorporate some of Babasaheb Ambedkar's ideas in it as well. What a good presentation that would make!

Back in the room, *Pedagogy of the Oppressed* seemed to be mocking him, lying half-open on the floor. There had been a time when he had believed in it, just as he had been carried away by Babasaheb

Ambedkar's ideas, reading his biography late into the night.

Dilip pushed *Pedagogy* under the bed with his foot. He wasn't supposed to touch books with his feet. Books were knowledge, hence sacred, not to be defiled. Well, since the Dalits had been created from God's feet, it made sense that he was now desecrating a book with his foot.

Dilip knew how Freire would have dealt with adversity. He would have gone out and mobilized people, people like himself, in a similar plight, and tried to bring pressure on the powers-that-be. Were there many people like himself? Dalit students who had won scholarships to pursue education that had been denied to them for centuries? He knew there were others like him even in Elphistone College, but he did not know them personally.

Here he was on a scholarship that had seemed enormous in Wadgav, but which didn't go very far in Bombay. He had learnt to make ends meet, if he got the money in the first place. Education for Dalits was one of the things Babasaheb Ambedkar had fought for. Ambedkar, Freire, his cousin Milind were different from him. They were strong. They had made it. He was alone. He had friends, family, yet he could not turn to them. There was no one who could help him, not Vishnu, not Malti, no one.

Maybe he should have a bath. He hadn't had a shower for 3-4 days and felt itchy. At least the showers would be free at this time of the night, though the water would be cold. Dilip passed his hand over his face to encounter a stubble. He had stopped shaving as well. What was the use of all that?

"Eh Dilip, *tu Devdas mat ban, yaar.*" *Don't be a tragic hero, my friend.* Vishnu had teased him yesterday, then hurriedly changed the subject. Dilip had become so cranky lately. There was no telling what might put him in a bad mood, even a harmless little joke could cause a bruise.

Were things that bad? Yes they were, for there was last week's sociology exam. He had prepared himself the best he could, even though he wasn't feeling very well and did not have complete notes. He had taken a seat in the second row in the exam hall. Prof. Wagle who was invigilating along with a female professor caught Dilip's eye and smiled. God knows how he felt about his frequent absence from class.

Dilip quickly scanned the question paper. He knew two questions well, he was O.K on two and rather shaky on the last one. He looked around him. People were settling down to write. Vishnu winked at him from the other end of the room.

Dilip took up his pen and started writing. He wrote half of the first answer when he was hit by a wave of dizziness. He put his pen down because his hand was trembling. What was the matter with him? He looked around the room; everyone was writing hard. The atmosphere was peaceful, with the occasional turning of a page, and the mechanical creaking of the ancient, ceiling fans.

Dilip took up his pen again but he couldn't concentrate. With great difficulty he finished the first question and started on the next. He felt really weird. His head felt light and heavy by turn, and soon he had a throbbing headache. He put down his pen and squinted at his answer paper, which wasn't quite in focus. He had to get out. He couldn't write any more. He might faint or something. He didn't want to make a fuss.

Prof. Wagle had got up from his seat and was walking around the classroom. He was at the other end of the room; it was a good time for Dilip to make his escape. He got up, pushed his pens into his pocket, willed himself to walk rapidly to the table and dropped his answer sheet there. Without looking back, he walked swiftly out of the room.

How was he ever going to face Prof. Wagle now? He had barely spent 30 minutes on the exam. Only third class students did that, or those who failed. He would never be able to go back to college again. Never.

His father had not got as far as college. He had finished secondary school, then worked at odd jobs in nearby towns, living away from the family, sending money home. Then he had got a job at the post office in the next village and had started living at home again. It was a steady, government job, a reservation job. Dilip's grandfather, barely literate, had toiled for next to nothing in other people's fields, and died young. And now he, Dilip, who had won a scholarship to go to Elphinstone College, was going to fail his mid-term Sociology exam.

He remembered a few lines by a Dalit poet. Vishnu had lent him books on Dalit poetry; the poems had moved him. They visited him sometimes, like this, when he was up at an unusual hour.

> *Mother, you used to tell me*
> *when I was born*
> *your labour was very long.*
> *The reason, mother,*
> *the reason for your long labour:*
> *I, still in your womb, was wondering*
> *Do I want to be born –*
> *Do I want to be born at all*
> *in this land?*

Dilip woke up late on Sunday morning. It was almost 11 a.m. when his eyes opened to a room full of light and sound. "*Meine tere liye hi saat raang ke sapne chune, sapne surile sapne …*" *I have chosen these seven-hued dreams just for you, these lyrical dreams …* Another Hindi film song was blaring from the transistor downstairs.

He had to get something to eat. Holding on to the iron frame, he sat up in bed with some effort. Brushing his teeth with the meagre bit of toothpaste that was left, he changed from his shirt into a t-shirt. Then he went downstairs.

Most people were grouped around the TV set watching the popular serial "Ramayan," which depicted a great Hindu epic. He was thankful that he did not have to talk to anyone.

"Hi Dilip," someone called out to him as he stepped out of the hostel compound. He managed a weak smile.

Weak, that's how he felt. The different parts of his body seemed to be loosely connected and walking normally had become something of an endeavour. Keeping his head down to avoid the glare of the sun, he walked over to the *maidan*. There weren't as many food sellers there today as on working days. So he had to wait his turn while they served other customers.

Finally Shyamlal, the *wada-pav walla*, turned to him. Dilip offered him the crumpled one-rupee note. "*Baki kal de dunga,*" he said. *I will pay you the rest tomorrow.* Shyamlal heated a bun on the *tava*, sliding a blob of oil under it. While the *wadas* were heating, he pulled the bun off the griddle, opened it and spread the red-hot, chili-garlic chutney on it.

Dilip's eyes closely followed Shyamlal's deft movements, while the smell of cheap, hot oil rising from the *tava* stung his senses. He carried his *wada-pav* to one end of the *maidan* and sat down on the grass. He wanted to eat carefully, so he wouldn't spill anything. The food inflamed his mouth, making his eyes water. His mouth was probably tender, his tongue a bit swollen.

Groups of young men in white pant-shirts and caps were playing cricket. Dilip watched the game near him as he ate. After he had finished, he wiped his hands on the grass. He felt better. He was still hungry, but felt stronger.

He made his way back to the hostel taking a small detour and going first to Churchgate station. Standing at the newspaper stand inside the station, he scanned headlines and examined magazine covers. He wanted to pick up the *Indian Express*, and read it, but he knew that the owner frowned upon people browsing through his wares without buying anything. The newspapers they got at the hostel would have disappeared by now. You had to get up early to get a shot at them.

Back in his room, Dilip sat down in his chair, which was turned towards the open balcony door. Maybe Vishnu would return later that day and he would borrow a few rupees from him. It would be wonderful to go and eat some *biryani* at Colaba. After all, he would be able to cash his cheque tomorrow and return the money.

But then again it was possible that Vishnu would come back only on Monday. Dilip regretted that he hadn't gone to Dahisar with him. Vishnu's cousin and wife were very nice people. They had two small children; Dilip enjoyed playing with them. Now there was nothing for him to do here but brood about the sociology exam. He wasn't going to do very well in economics and political science either. But at least he would scrape through in those subjects.

He couldn't dream any more about a conversation with Professor Wagle and the presentation on Freire. The Prof. would be completely disgusted with Dilip after he saw the exam. Perhaps he should have told him that he was sick. He might have had a re-exam then. But he didn't want to give the exam again, anyway. He was really, truly fucked, as Vishnu would have put it.

As the day wore on, Dilip wished more and more that he had gone with Vishnu. Vishnu was his only real friend in hard, ungiving Bombay. Dilip wouldn't have survived all this time, without him.

He tried all day to read his notes, so he could figure out what bits were missing, but his mind refused to focus. He had a little more success cleaning his room.

He found Pradeep's number, scrawled on a chit, as he was sorting through his papers. He should call him, but not today. He knew that he was expected to get involved in the marriage preparations. There wasn't much time left. Malti's wedding was going to be held in Bombay at some expense. Where would he get the money to give her a nice wedding present? He wanted to feel enthusiastic about the wedding, energized about Malti living in Bombay. But all he felt was dread at being at an event as public and vociferous as a wedding, with hundreds of garishly dressed guests, kinetic kids getting in the way and a hired band playing loud music.

By evening, Vishnu still hadn't returned. He wouldn't come now till the next day. He wished he had Vishnu's cousin's phone number. He desperately wanted to talk to someone. He knew the cousin's last name and the street he lived on, so he could probably look him up in the directory. But there was no point in calling Vishnu. He would get worried; he might even interrupt his visit and rush back to the hostel. Vishnu was always worrying about him, as it was. He had been talking about getting in touch with Dilip's parents, telling Dilip that he needed to go home and rest, eat. But Dilip had managed to dissuade him, telling him he would go to Wadgav soon, in the summer holidays.

Dilip shut his door against the sounds of the Sunday evening TV film, emanating from the common room downstairs, and lay down on the bed. All he had to do was get through somehow to the next morning. Then he would cash the cheque and eat. The idea didn't stir him at all. He felt like banging his head against the wall. If only he had the energy to do it! The thought frightened him. Maybe he should go down and watch the film? Anything to escape his own mind.

Suddenly he wished that he could be angry, feel righteous, believe that the world owed him something. A meal. A job. Dignity. He tried to recall Vishnu's words about the plight of the Dalits. He wanted to remember Ambedkar's speeches. He wanted to hear Vishnu recite Dalit poems with feeling and expression. He yearned to talk about Freire's masterful explanation on how oppression worked, in a dazzling presentation. But, but he could not. He couldn't do any of it.

His mind was weary, blank, as he continued to sit on his chair. How long had he been sitting there? He could not tell.

He was sinking into a huge hopelessness, overturned by a tsunami of self loathing, a despair that was deep, dark and final. As a sob rose to his throat, he buried his face in the pillow. Harsh sobs filled the room. Then they abruptly stopped. He felt a sense of release. He was floating, hovering in mid-air, with only a slight consciousness of the weight and mass of his body.

Dilip lay down on his bed and switched off the light. He dozed and dreamt that Freire had come to

Bombay. The ministers and the VIP's were at the air-port to receive him. Freire stepped out of the plane. Standing at the top of the folding stairs, he smiled and waved to the crowd. People rushed forward to greet him as he walked down the steps.

A beautiful girl in a silk *saree* placed a garland of marigolds around Freire's neck. Another girl put a red *tikka* on his forehead. More people surrounded him, garlands in hand. Then Dilip was at the hostel, getting ready in a hurry, to go and listen to a talk Freire was giving. He ran downstairs, to be stopped by the doorman. There was a riot outside, he was told; the streets were unsafe.

He paced the hostel corridor waiting for the riot to end. It was getting late. Finally he decided to go out anyway. He stepped out of the hostel gate. A stone flew at him out of nowhere and hit the gatepost. Dilip ducked and stepped back into the compound. The doorman shut the gate after him.

Then Dilip fell into a deeper sleep from which he awoke a little after midnight. He was sweating, fear-ful, a band of tension stretched tight across his chest. He lay feeling groggy and disoriented for some time. Then he sat up and switched on the table lamp.

The street was dark and quiet. Holding on to the cool, balcony railing, shivering a little, Dilip looked down at the stone slabs, four floors below. All he had to do was hoist himself up and push his body into space. He had tried it once – was it last week, or the week before that? – and found it quite hard to do. He had managed to get high above the railing, balancing on his hands, his feet clear off the floor. But he hadn't really intended to jump then.

The image of Malti in a white nurse's uniform, most of her hair hidden under the starched cap, flashed through Dilip's mind. Malti would make a good nurse; his parents would be proud of her.

He tried to hoist himself up on the balcony railing, his heart slamming against his ribs, his mouth open, gasping with the effort. It was too tough. He felt so weak. He sat down in the balcony, on the cool, dusty floor, and rested his head against the wall. He stayed like that for a while, his mind in a daze. Then he got up and tried again. This time he succeeded. With his body jutting out of the balcony, into the night, he looked down again.

What was he going to do with himself this time?

Dilip pushed himself out, into space.

Absolution

The alarm rang. Half asleep, Ashok switched it off and stayed put. He could faintly hear Nilima pottering around in the kitchen. Now she padded into the darkened bedroom. "You'll be late Ashok," she said, in Marathi, their mother tongue.

Ashok opened his eyes and looked at his smiling wife. He had never been able to appreciate the fact that she looked so fresh, first thing in the morning. He was only two years ahead, but looked at least five years older. He had aged suddenly over the last year, when his company's orders had soared and his heart had taken the plunge.

Feeling a bit groggy, he got out of bed and walked to the bathroom. He avoided the mirror as he brushed his teeth. His eyes were puffy and reddish in the mornings, as if he had been out drinking with his buddies the night before.

Wearing old shorts and a faded t-shirt, Ashok walked into the dining room, decorated with beautiful, flowering plants. There were plants everywhere in the darn house. Their small garden couldn't accommodate Nilima's love for growing things.

Sashwati was already seated at the dining table, wearing a flower-patterned salwar-kameez, hair tied up in a bouncy pony-tail.

"All set?" she asked.

"You make it sound like we're going for a game of tennis," said Ashok grumpily. He would have preferred a family of late-risers who got out of bed feeling foul. Instead he had a sunrise-worshipping wife and her niece, Sashwati, who practiced yoga every morning.

"It's not like tennis but you do sweat a bit," Sashwati said in her cheerful voice. Ashok did not bother to say anything. How would they ever know how utterly good it felt to crouch on one side of a net, purposefully gripping a racquet, waiting for the ball, ready, in every sense of the term, to meet your opponent?

"Where's my tea?" he asked instead.

Nilima was busy watering the plants in the kitchen garden.

"You're not supposed to have tea before class, remember?" Sashwati said.

"I don't normally, but I feel like it today."

"You said you wanted to do everything properly."

"You said I should strictly follow the rules. Wasn't my idea. Missing my morning tea, that's too much."

Nilima, who could hear everything through the open door, put down the watering can and came into the room. She laid her hand gently on Ashok's shoulder.

"Please, let's not have an argument first thing," she said in Marathi, looking at him with her large, soulful eyes. "I can make you tea, but then you'll be late."

"I don't want to be late," Sashwati said. "I'll take a rickshaw."

Ashok and Sashwati sat silently in the car, as Ashok drove to the yoga centre, sans tea. How good they were, these two, at making him feel bad. He should not have agreed to go for yoga, but Dr. Khare had been so insistent.

Old man Khare would have never made such demands. He would have just written out a prescription and advised Ashok to reduce stress, leaving the means to him. He had been their family doctor for 20 years. After he retired, his son Ramesh had taken over, with new-fangled ideas he had picked up in the U.S. Ramesh even quoted Deepak Chopra, that fraud. For god's sake, it was one thing for the Americans to go gaga over Chopra, but Indians should know better.

Ashok would have preferred going back to tennis. He had played the game, three times a week, for many years. Then his business had got too busy and he had had a heart attack.

Dr. Khare had passed his practice on to his son and retired happily, but Ashok couldn't do that. He and Nilima had no children, though there was Sashwati.

Nilima's elder sister had lost her husband when Sashwati was very young. All she could find was a low-paying, secretarial job. They had naturally helped out with Sashwati's education. Not that it cost much to put a girl through a Marathi-medium school and get her started on her B.A. in Marathi Literature.

Ashok had wanted her to go to an English-medium, which would improve her chances, but his sister-in-law was having none of that. And in college he wanted her to do science or commerce. Or economics, at least, finishing up with an MBA. He had spoken to Sashwati a few times, but she was firm about her plans. She wanted to work in publishing. She was already doing some freelance editing for a children's book publisher. Ashok's successful business, manufacturing precision medical instruments, would die with him, or be sold off.

After the heart attack, Sashwati had brought up yoga. And Ramesh Khare, all polish and posh accent, had talked about how cost effective yoga was compared to all other stress reduction techniques. Ashok had wanted to tell him that money was no problem, but had held back out of respect for the older Dr. Khare. Sashwati had spent weeks extolling the virtues of yoga and Nilima *mavshi*, her aunt, had backed her gently but firmly. Finally, Ashok had relented.

Well, it didn't matter very much. He would do yoga for a few more weeks to please them all, then give up and return to tennis. His heart attack had been quite mild. He had been denied the pleasure of boasting that he had survived a triple bypass, like his school friend, Sandeep.

He would give up Dr. Ramesh Khare too if need be. He wasn't going to be pushed around by everyone, especially not a 19-year-old niece.

Ashok glanced at her, sitting upright beside him in the passenger seat. Catching his look, she said: "Maybe we should pick up some *idlis* for breakfast on our way home." Yes, reward me for my suffering with fluffy *idlis*, hot-hot *sambar* and creamy *coconut chutney*, Ashok thought. Bribe me.

He recalled what Khanna, at his office, had said: "No doubt you feel good at the end of yoga, Sir. You tie yourself up in impossible knots that generate so much pain that you are glad when it's over."

Nilima would go on her morning walk with her friend, Kasturi, while they were doing yoga. They would take a few rounds in the large, well-maintained public garden near their house, stop to smell flowers, enjoy the relative coolness of the morning, exchange smiles with other neighbours out for their morning constitutional, buy green mangoes on their way home. How was it that Nilima had never opted for yoga?

There were some 20 people in the class, which was held in a large room, the floor covered with thick rugs. The many windows were flung open to salute the sun well, no doubt, thought Ashok. Why, in a country like India, where the sun burnt people to a crisp every summer, would you want to do *suryana-maskar* – the sun salutation? People died in droves in heat waves every year. Better to invest in air conditioning than sing hymns to the god-awful tropical sun. Yes they had done that thousands of years ago, according to the *Rigveda*, but how was it relevant today?

Anandita, the teacher, was at the other end of the room, talking to one of the students. Today she wore black tights and a fitting red t-shirt. Ashok could not help staring at her Bo Derek figure. He had been unprepared to meet someone like Anandita on the first day of class. He rarely recalled women's clothing, but he had no trouble remembering what she had worn – gold tights and a purple T-shirt.

"I am so glad you're joining our class, Mr. Muthe," she had said, clasping his hand in a firm handshake. He had been expecting a *namaste*. "You're really going to enjoy it. And you have Sash to help you along. She's one of my best students."

I have done very well for myself all these years without Sash's help, thought Ashok. Really, the whole thing was getting absurd. He had seen Sashwati as a snotty baby dressed only in her *chaddi*, and now she was going to help him with yoga.

"Let's take our places," Anandita said. "We'll speak again after the class."

Ashok sat down cross-legged, rather uncomfortably, on the very last rug in the room. Sashwati took the rug in front of him, turning around to give him a reassuring smile before sitting down with her legs folded in a perfect *padmasan, the lotus pose.*

First they said "Om" three times, then a *shlok,* a hymn, in Sanskrit, which took Ashok back to his childhood. His paternal grandfather had taught him several *shloks* and how to do the daily *puja, the* Hindu religious ritual, when he was five. His grandparents had died a couple of years later.

For his secondary school Ashok had been sent to an elite, public school in Darjeeling. His father, who was in the army, wanted a modern, high-class, English education for his only son. His parents didn't want to move him from school to school every two years when his father got his transfer orders. His mother came often to visit him in Darjeeling, staying for weeks in a hotel.

Ashok liked the sound of the Sanskrit verses, wishing he knew what they meant. Perhaps Sashwati would be able to tell him. Maybe he would ask her later. Maybe the yoga class would turn out okay after all.

The prayer was followed by several stretching exercises, done in slow motion. It's been a while since I even stretched my hands above my head, thought Ashok. Bending forward, he realized that his paunch was larger than expected; he had put on five kilos in the past year.

There was no avoiding the *suryanamaskar* that came next. He found himself a bit out of breath on the fourth one. They usually did seven at a stretch.

"Don't strain yourself. Do only as much as you can do naturally."

Anandita's voice floated out to Ashok. She must do aerobics or something, he thought. You couldn't possibly get that muscle tone with yoga.

"Let your hands rest by your sides. Keep your back straight and close your eyes if you like. Feel your heart rate gradually slowing down. Always be aware of what's going on in your body. Be aware of your breath, moving in and out, in and out, effortlessly."

Anandita's speech was deliberately slow and even, her voice soothing.

How his body had ached the first few days after that class. It was unbelievable, the effect a bit of stretching and bending could have. But he had got used to it, and he had to admit that yoga made him feel rather good.

A strange thing had happened two weeks into the class. He had begun remembering some of his dreams. It was not exactly a blessing. Many of his dreams centred around trains – going to meet someone at the station, being seen off as he undertook a long journey, preparing to board trains, missing trains, and being robbed en route. Could his mother's fear of train robberies have somehow got to him, lingering in his subconscious long after her death?

Once someone had snatched his mother's gold chain, through the train window, just as the train was leaving the platform. The incident traumatized her. Given the frequent transfers, she had to pack their belongings and take them on trains with her, every so often. She would always become very anxious as the moving date approached.

Ashok's grandmother had no sympathy for her daughter's fears. "Why do you worry, you silly thing, when you have a Commander for a husband?" she would say.

Ashok's mother did not see her husband in a heroic role. He wasn't always armed, but the dacoits would be, she said. Armed with rifles, with a garland of bullets hanging down from their thick, bullish necks.

Their faces would be covered in soiled bandanas, revealing nothing but their small, cruel eyes, glittering malevolently. Dacoit images from Bollywood movies haunted her dreams as well.

In the early days of their marriage, Nilima had often asked Ashok about his dreams, and he had been at a loss to recall them. Then Nilima would start talking about her dreams, dreams about river crossings, bathing *ghats* along a sacred river dotted with shrines, crones who accosted her as she emerged from a temple, telling her to perform this or that ritual to secure the well-being of her family.

Ashok half listened to these tales, sitting with the morning paper open before him. As his wife spoke, he stole glances at the headlines, eager to read the sports page, then politics and business. There was something solid and reassuring about a cricket match between England and India, or the defection of a prominent politician from the Janata to the Congress, or the rise and fall of stocks. Here was the world, perhaps not in the best shape, but one that could be depended upon. What was one to make of the shadowy world of dreams with its slippery meanings?

Ashok took his preferred spot in class, near a window, not far from the front wall, which was dominated by a large image of Lord Ganesh. He had an important meeting at 11 a.m., which he needed to prepare for. He had time. He must focus on the poses, still his mind, so that when they finally got to *shavasan*, the corpse pose, he would be totally relaxed.

As they waited at the Udipi Restaurant to have their *idlis* packed, Ashok downed a quick *chai*. Sashwati refused tea because she was keeping a *vrat*.

"What?" Ashok said. "You're keeping a vow? Why? What foolishness will you think of next?"

Sashwati merely smiled.

"So what is the *vrat* for?"

Sashwati remained silent.

"Well?" Ashok persisted.

"I'll tell you later," she said.

"You're not in trouble, are you?"

"No."

"I can help if there's a problem. If you need some money ..."

"No, no, I'm fine."

Ashok decided to drop it for the moment.

Sashwati was a strange girl. Why didn't she paint her nails, giggle over boys and watch MTV, like the rest of them?

"Because she is Sashwati," Nilima said, with obvious pride in the girl she had helped her sister bring up.

True there was nothing negative about Sashwati; she was helpful, happy and purposive. But that was just it. Wasn't such equanimity unnatural at her age? She even made frequent visits to the temple near their house.

The ritual had started when her maternal grandmother, who lived with Ashok and Nilima, became too feeble to go on her own. Sashwati used to come by then, take her grandmother by hand, and bring her to the temple, both walking at a snail's pace. That was somewhat understandable; it was sweet of her to take on this chore. But her grandmother had passed away a year ago, and Sashwati still went to the temple. And now this, this vow!

When he got home, the maid informed him that Nilima had come and gone out again. As Ashok made his way towards the bathroom, his eyes fell on the old black and white family photographs lined up on a shelf in the living room. There was Nilima

– youthful, smiling a trifle shyly, her hair in braids – a slightly out of focus photo from her college days.

Through the 20 years of their marriage, arranged by Ashok's aunt, Nilima had astonished him with her adaptability, her range. She read *Time* and *Asiaweek* that he subscribed to, and discussed world politics with him. She watched Wimbledon and cricket with him on TV. She entertained his business buddies at home, assembling great meals with the help of their cook. She wore beautiful, silk *sarees* to work-related parties, or business dinners at fancy restaurants, and seemed at home there. She grew prize-winning roses. Twice a month, she went to a class with her sister, where they read and interpreted the *Bhagwat Geeta*. Once a month, she went to a village near Pune, to help a friend out with a women's literacy project.

What is she, if not the perfect wife, Ashok thought as he turned on the shower. True they had no children, but the fault lay with his low sperm count. After the tests, they had talked about adoption for a while, but nothing had materialized.

He wondered if he had been a good husband. A heck of a question, yet it deserved some reflection.

He didn't want to ask Nilima how he ranked as a husband. And even if he did, would he get an answer, let alone an honest one? She would probably just laugh it off.

Vigorously towelling himself down, Ashok compiled a list of traits that cast him in a favourable light: he encouraged Nilima in whatever she wanted to do, admired her roses and her culinary efforts, bought her a new *saree* a couple of times a year, gave her expensive jewellery and perfume on her birthday. She was rarely sick, but when she was, he tried to come home early from work. He saw to it that the car and driver were at her disposal on the days she went to the village for the literacy project. He was always courteous towards her relatives, particularly her sister. He had provided well for her materially, though she did not ask for much. The house and a generous proportion of shares were in her name. She would have no problems financially if he succumbed to a sudden heart attack.

Two days passed before he brought up the subject of the vow again. He felt that he had to get to the bottom of it. Sashwati was unusual, but taking a religious vow was going too far. He needed to know what it was all about. After all, he was her guardian. He decided to approach the issue while driving home after yoga.

"What does it involve, this vow of yours?" he asked.

"No tea or coffee," she said. "Meat I don't eat anyway. Eggs are not allowed either."

Well, he thought, at least she's talking today.

"So what's the idea?"

"The main thing is to keep the mind calm and pure. There's a prayer every night before going to bed and one after waking up, at dawn, and there's a ceremony, once a month. On a full moon night, I must go to a *Peepal* tree and do a *puja* under it."

A cold hand clutched at Ashok's heart.

"I must make certain offerings, say a prayer, then collect my offerings and bury them in the ground. Through all this I must be totally silent."

"And what do you offer?" he asked hoarsely.

Sashwati cast him an odd look. "Half a coconut, a betel nut, flowers, milk, rice, a few *tulsi* leaves ..." Her voice trailed off.

They were on the main road, in the thick of traffic.

"You're holding back on me, Sashwati," he said angrily. "You're holding back on the main offering."

"Watch out!" Sashwati squealed as a scooter suddenly appeared in front of the car.

Ashok swerved just in time to avoid it and swerved again to miss the pavement.

"Arre, arre, kya karta hai?" a man on a cycle yelled out. *Hey, what are you doing?*

He had managed to avoid an accident, but he was not done with her yet, not by a far shot.

Gripped by the same determination that had helped him win tennis matches with Sandeep every now and then, even though Sandeep was a much better player, he turned the car into a side street and parked near a big, overflowing garbage bin.

Turning to a visibly nervous Sashwati, he said: "So?"

Sashwati said nothing, staring straight ahead through the windshield, her hands clenched in her lap.

"What's missing from the picture is menstrual blood, right?"

Still no answer.

"This is a ritual you do when you lose a child, right?"

Sashwati nodded slightly, still not looking at him.

"And you learnt about this from your aunt?"

Sashwati did not answer.

What unholy things were going on? Why was Sashwati enacting a ritual that Nilima had also performed, years ago, in her dreams? Had she got pregnant and had abortion or something? Sashwati, of all people!

"Why are you doing it?" Ashok demanded, his voice rising. "Tell me why."

Suddenly, Sashwati turned and looked steadily at him. She seemed to have come to a decision. Taking the bottle of water that they kept in the car, she took a couple of swigs and offered it to him. Ashok ignored it.

"Ashok *kaka, uncle,* you want to hear the whole story?" she asked in Marathi.

He nodded.

"Did you know *Aai, mother,* was pregnant after me?" she asked.

"Yes. Your mother had a miscarriage, no?"

"Not really. *Aai* went away to Aurangabad for the last few months of the pregnancy. Do you remember that?"

"Sort of."

"*Aai* was having a tough pregnancy. So in the seventh month she left me with granny and went to Aurangabad to be with her gynaecologist friend there. The baby was born soon after, premature, but also with Down's Syndrome. It was a boy. He was given away to an orphanage. *Aai* felt she could not look after him. Papa had died four months before; I was just two; and *Aai* did not have a job."

Sashwati stopped to drink more water.

"*Aai* went back to the orphanage later and made inquiries. My brother was adopted when he was one. They have no records of who took him."

"Can I have some?" asked Ashok, reaching for the bottle. What he really needed was a strong cup of tea. A stiff peg of scotch would be even better.

Sashwati passed him the bottle.

"How did you find out all this?" he asked.

"I overheard ma and Nilima *mavshi* – bits and pieces here and there. One day I begged *Aai* to tell me everything, and she did."

Nilima had not told him all this. All he had heard were accounts of the dreams, and he had retreated from them behind the pages of *The Times of India.* If his memory served him right, the dreams had taken

place around the same time as the supposed miscarriage. He wondered if Nilima would have told him
about her sister's plight if he had paid more attention.
How had Nilima learnt of the ritual? Maybe her sister
had considered doing it upon giving up the boy?

"So why are you keeping the vow?" he asked.

"*Aai* is still not fully reconciled to giving up the
baby. She feels a bit bad about it. That's what she told
Nilima *mavshi* and *mavshi* tried to console her. Then
I came across this book, a funny, old book, among
aaji's, grandmother's, things. It had these strange drawings and it talked about this ritual. You know one of
aaji's friends is still alive? She comes every day to the
temple. I talk to her sometimes. One day I told her
everything and showed her the book, and she told me
to keep the vow. I thought about it for weeks. It was
kind of weird. But I decided to give it a try. Maybe
there could be something, you know, like absolution.
Maybe *aai* would feel better."

"Absolution ... that's a big word."

Ashok looked affectionately at Sashwati. What a
wonderful girl she was. They did not need their own
child; they had one.

"The old lady thought it was a really good idea,"
she mumbled.

"And your aunt and mother, do they know about
this?"

Sashwati shook her head.

"You expect me to keep it secret?"

"Yes, please."

Ashok started the car. She was still a child. So trust-
ing. *Yes, please.* Nothing could be that simple. Just
hide it all from your wife, will you? Innocent of the
intimacies of marriage and of the evasions. Innocent
of the fact that absolution is granted to the sinner, not

the proxy. But in this case he was going to make it as simple as those two little words: *Yes, please.*

"No more *vrats* after you complete this one, okay?" he said.

"No more *vrats*," she said, smiling a little. "I do find it a bit spooky. But … I think it's all right. I trust the old lady."

"Promise?" Ashok said, extending his upturned palm towards her.

"Promise," she said, smiling hugely and making a small, pinching movement on his palm.

After a while he said: "I think you should go for that hiking trip to the Valley of Flowers. You were talking about it a lot last year. I would be happy to sponsor it."

"Oh, that would be fantastic!" Sashwati cried. "I'm sure Mandira would come too. Thank you, *kaka*."

Some things he would never really know: how his wife rated him as a husband; what his sister-in-law had gone through in giving up her misshapen son; why his dreams featured runaway trains. But one thing was clear, as an uncle he had done his good deed for the day.

Smoke and Mirrors

I could plunge the knife right through her heart, thought Kavita, cold and clear, quick and clean.

She looked at her friend lying back on the plush, leather chair, which had been converted into a recliner by the girl who was attending to her. Shanti's eyes were covered with cotton pads dipped in a cucumber concoction, supposedly to cool and cleanse them. Her round, fair face was smeared with a thick, lime-green paste, the garish lighting in the beauty parlour accentuating the weird effect. The white sheet that draped her large, middle-aged frame fell just short of her swollen-looking feet, incongruously encased in flimsy, golden sandals.

Kavita recalled giving them to her. After buying them, she had decided that she didn't like them. This happened to her often. Shanti always wore the clothes, jewellery or accessories she received from Kavita; the reverse, however, did not hold.

Kavita ached for a cigarette. But she too was a prisoner of the avocado-aloe facemask that was the latest in skin firming from Paris. The parlour owner had gushed about its properties when they had first got there. Besides, the parlour had lately banned smoking. She tried to relax in her comfortable chair, but last night's drama passed yet again through her mind.

She and Avinash had been on their way home, after a business dinner with some Japanese clients. They had had a little too much to drink and were lying back half dozing, in the backseat of the Mercedes that their driver drove through the streets of late-night Delhi, when Kavita's cell phone rang.

It was Shanti, calling to tell her that Ravi, Shanti's son, had got 96 percent in the all-important secondary school examinations. Kavita hung up after congratulating Shanti. Turning to Avinash, she gave him the good news. Avinash seemed to startle out of his alcoholic slumber and sit upright, but he remained silent.

Back home Kavita greeted Mehul, their son, who has just come in rather early, she thought. On her way to the bedroom to change, she saw Avinash fixing himself a drink at the bar. Minutes later, his livid face loomed in the dressing table mirror. She looked questioningly at him, as he glared at her, saying nothing at first.

"It's great isn't it, for Shanti and Ram," he said, finally, his voice low but furious, as she turned around to face him. "But what about us?" Then he screamed suddenly: "Ravi will get into IIT. Go to the U.S.A. and do an MBA at a top school. And Mehul? Mehul will rot here."

Kavita leapt to her feet and ran to shut the bedroom door. Most likely Mehul was in his room with his door closed and headphones on, but he might still be in the living room, within earshot.

"What kind of mother are you?" Avinash continued in a high voice. "You ruined Mehul's life."

Kavita stared at her normally sedate husband in shock.

"And Shanti, you know what Shanti's done? Shanti has done everything for Ravi. Everything."

Then he turned and left the room, slamming the door after him.

"I think I fell asleep. That face massage was so nice," Shanti said, rousing Kavita from her thoughts. She smiled at Kavita through the mirror. Shanti had a radiant smile, a luminosity that had intensified since she had become a devotee of that godman, a few years ago.

Kavita quickly closed her eyes; she didn't want Shanti to see her expression. The girl took a sponge to her face and Kavita gave herself up to its pleasure. She sighed and pictured that other hand caressing her neck, moving slowly downward. She would only see him next week. Not soon enough, but there was no other way to arrange it.

Last night ... she was back again, sitting before the dressing table, the mirror reflecting a slim, attractive, brown-skinned woman with a hint of lines around the eyes and the mouth. Automatically, she had started removing her make-up again, her mind suspended between comprehension and incredulity.

Avinash had come in to say that he would sleep that night at the family mansion. He had talked in his normal voice, not really looking at her, before walking out again. He had never done that before, not in all the seven years since they had left the joint-family mansion, that warren of intrigues where Kavita's mother-in-law had reigned supreme.

The night had been interminable. Scenes from her life – mixed up and out-of-order – passed through her consciousness, a projector that could not be switched off. Avinash at the college fashion show, she in that shimmering, midnight blue *shalwaar kameez*; her first little modelling assignment. At the airport with her sister Aditi, Aditi saying over and over that she would send for Kavita as soon as she got her

Green Card. The news of her parents in the car accident, the mangled bodies never actually seen, but surfacing, over and over, in nightmares. Clinging to her grandmother, crying, while her grandmother sat unmoving, remote, mute in the depths of her grief. Telling her mother-in-law she was pregnant and having her come running to embrace her, for the first time ever. Avinash proposing to her late one night at the Oberoi Grand coffee shop, looking so soulful, so sincere; a mix of elation and confusion rising in her.

Stop, she whispered, stop, but the images continued to roll. As the night deepened, the pictures started losing their sharp edges, slurring and stumbling like a drunk, and a profound fatigue finally dragged her down into the blankness of sleep.

She woke up late, got painfully out of bed, made herself coffee and started looking around for a cigarette. She had quit a few months ago. The clock was ticking; Shanti would arrive soon to pick her up for their monthly pilgrimage to the parlour.

She found a few cigarettes in an old pack. Avinash called just as she lit one, telling her that he was going for a game of golf with his brother and would be back for dinner. Just that, nothing more.

"We need to talk," she said.

"Yes, tonight," he responded, before hanging up.

Kavita sat down at the dining table. Avinash had slapped her last night, slapped her, humiliated her, shamed her, stepped all over her. He had accomplished all of that in minutes, with mere words. It was the language of battering that explained what had transpired. It was how they said it in the soaps and tabloids. He had slapped her, and on top of that, he showed no remorse.

She wanted to fling the mug in her hand, with full force, at the wall; wanted to watch it break and have coffee dribbling down the newly painted, ochre surface.

He owed her an apology for the unjust accusations he had flung her way, and oh so casually. He needed to seek her forgiveness. Instead he had made a curt phone call. The vileness of anger, which started way down in her gut, rose swiftly to her mouth.

"Hey mom." Mehul came in and sat down at the table. "What's up?"

Kavita looked at her son's handsome, square jawed face. His arms in a fitting, short-sleeved t-shirt were muscled from working out. A lock of curly hair fell over one eye. He was a picture of relaxed, casually virile youth, and her heart warmed to him.

"Nothing much," she said.

"Where's dad?"

"Gone golfing."

"Good. He needs the exercise."

"Don't you get too clever now," said Kavita, getting up, pretending to box his ears.

Mehul caught her hands, grinning.

He's a perfectly normal boy, Kavita thought, as she slipped into a pair of jeans. There was nothing wrong with Mehul. He went to discos, in fact he even DJ'd sometimes. He loved his music collection, his guitar and his mo-bike. He hung out with his friends. He didn't study much, that was true. It was understood that he would join Avinash's company and learn the ropes there. He wasn't stupid; he would figure out the business once he started working. What did Avinash expect? All Avinash had was a BA in Economics, same as her. Ravi had always been a scholar, and he was Ram's son. Ram, Shanti's husband, had an MBA from UCLA.

"Kavita, are you okay?" Shanti asked, as soon as she saw her.

"Bad night," Kavita replied.

"You're working too hard," Shanti said. "The sale was wonderful, but it was a lot of work, wasn't it?"

Shanti had come, of course, to the annual summer novelties show and sale at Kavita's boutique. She had asked Kavita weeks ahead if she could help in any way. She had run last-minute errands, and come early, nicely dressed, with trays of sweets from a well-known sweet shop in Old Delhi. Avinash and Ram had just put in perfunctory appearances.

Kavita slumped against the seat of the car and closed her eyes; the bright sun was hurting them. She felt too tired to reach for her sunglasses. She would rest a few moments before lighting a cigarette. Shanti would notice that she had started smoking again, but what the hell.

What a goody-goody bitch! Shanti was like an impossibly virtuous heroine from those insufferable Indian epics. Or those eternally self-sacrificing creatures from old Bollywood movies that had now made their way into nauseating TV serials. Perfect daughter, perfect mother, perfect friend, perfect wife. Ah, but she wasn't quite the perfect wife, Kavita had found that out. Sitting up, she reached inside her purse and fished out a cigarette; she really must buy a fresh pack. Shanti looked at her, wide-eyed.

"It's too much," Kavita said. "I just have to."

"It's okay," Shanti said softly.

It's okay, when you have a son like Ravi and a husband like Ram, Kavita thought, inhaling deeply. It's more than okay, it's great. It's easy when you're allowed to bring up your own child. It's horrible when your mother-in-law watches your every move, and servants and relatives take your child out of your hands, pampering and spoiling him. And you have a husband who is too gutless to say anything to them, but not too spineless to hit out at you.

Kavita turned away from Shanti's serene face, with a hint of concern on it. Then, suddenly, it occurred to her that she held the trump card. Oh God, of course she did! She could bring Shanti down with a few, choice phrases, if she wanted to. Where would all that goodness be then, that radiance that came from chanting hymns and doing everything for her son?

I am more beautiful and resourceful than her, Kavita thought. She had triumphed despite the despotic mother-in-law and the weakling husband. She had managed to start her own home decor boutique and make a success of it. Her mother-in-law, who had frowned upon her working for someone else, as she put it, had been amenable to the boutique. She had even been proud of Kavita, had promoted the shop among her wealthy friends, and provided capital when she wanted to buy the shop next door and expand the business. At that point they still lived in the family mansion. Later, when her mother-in-law passed away, Kavita had finally been able to persuade Avinash to move out.

"What nail polish would you like madam?" The girl had finished removing the face mask and was setting up the side table for the pedicure. Kavita chose a shade from a tray crowded with sparkly little bottles. She looked around as the girl started on her feet.

Posters of ultra blonde, tight-skinned women, their blouses unbuttoned to show the right amount of cleavage, their hair fussed and teased into place, all sporting the same, fake, dazzling smile, stared down at her from the walls. And there were the Bollywood bimbos, trying, somewhat unsuccessfully, to ape the made-in-California wonders. Or should that be horrors?

Shanti was sitting on the sofa against the wall, flipping through some magazines, waiting for Kavita to finish. Shanti only had a facial done these days. She did not use nail polish anymore. She wore no makeup, except for some kohl, which emphasized her large, expressive eyes. She allowed a few streaks of greying hair to show; Kavita used henna on hers.

Shanti just comes for the company, Kavita suddenly realized. Their Sunday morning beauty ritual was always followed by lunch at the Club. It was the only time that she and Shanti really met. Kavita was busy with her boutique, entertaining Avinash's clients, going to the gym, and a 100 other things. Shanti had her guru, and her life. At first she had invited Kavita to the *satsangs, pujas* and talks, but getting no response, she had stopped.

They had spent a lot of time together as young brides, had supported each other through their pregnancies and all those things that babies go through – teething, tumbles, sudden fevers. Shanti had had an arranged marriage, Kavita's was a love match, but motherhood, the great leveller, had brought them to the same place.

Ravi was born a year before Mehul. Motherhood had been good for Shanti: her step became firmer, her softness manifested as strength and her quietness acquired a compelling depth. She was a self-assured mother who knew exactly what to do when. She exuded happiness when she was caring for Ravi, and Ravi in turn looked healthy and content. Kavita had marvelled at the change, a change that everyone remarked on – Avinash, Ram and her mother-in-law.

Mehul's birth had the opposite effect. After the delivery, Kavita entered a strange, apathetic state. She stopped arguing with her mother-in-law, and gave up trying to carve a life for herself amid the undistinguished mass of in-laws who she felt could never be her kin. Day in and day out, she sat before the TV, which she had hardly ever switched on before, and let them bring meals up to her room. The baby was mostly attended to by servants, her mother-in-law and an unmarried sister-in-law.

And yet, sometimes when she looked at Mehul, a flame would ignite within her. She would seize the baby, bury her face in his firm, warm belly, inhale his milky fragrance, tickle his pretty, little feet, suckle him at her breasts and rock him, crooning. The sounds that escaped from her lips when she held him tight, sounds of a wounded animal, scared her.

Shanti came to see her practically every day, with Ravi, bringing a gaily coloured quilt for Mehul, advice on which cough syrup worked best, and the latest magazines and video cassettes. She would suggest going out and, when Kavita demurred, she would insist. They drove often to the Lodi Gardens and took a walk, with the babies in their prams. Or they went to an ice-cream parlour where Shanti ordered extravagant creations like pistachio and butterscotch with caramel sauce. Joking and laughing like carefree teenagers, they scooped up the sickly sweet treat.

Shanti agreed with Kavita that Mehul was the most beautiful baby ever to be born, more beautiful even than Ravi, and urged her to go shopping for him, take him every day to the little park near the mansion and start researching play schools, even though it was a bit early for that.

As Kavita flipped through the magazines, stood on the balcony looking out at the traffic beyond the garden, showered to get ready for Shanti, she started becoming aware, once again, of the colours, shapes and textures of the world. Their vividness and intensity dazzled her. She noticed, as if for the first time, the fine filigree of the gold ornaments in the glossy magazine ads, the boldness of the block prints on the curtains that were all the rage in high-class, capital homes right then, the shocking pinks and peacock blues of the chudidar sets, trimmed with silver borders, and most of all, the luscious, mouth watering hues of make-up, which she had eschewed for many months.

At the Lodi Gardens, she was struck by the trilling bird song, the vastness of the cloudless sky that arched overhead, the sparseness of the wilting grass of late summer, the thick haze of heat, layer upon layer of it, which their bodies sliced through with the fluidity of fish gliding through water. Ancient Moghul tombs towered impressively above them, solid stone, turning amber at dusk. Kavita was filled with wonder at human ingenuity, thousands of years of it, and felt that she too must do something; must somehow leave a mark, however small, on the world.

It was then that the idea of a decor shop started to take shape in her mind, and she threw herself into the research with a frenzy that she had not experienced since her college days, when she had aimed at getting high marks in all her assignments and exams, and succeeded. And so she had set it up, with Shanti beside her, always ready to drive to yet another factory outlet in the suburbs, Avinash wordlessly writing out cheques, her mother-in-law beaming approval, and Mehul gambolling in her lap, when she came home flushed and excited from her endeavours.

Kavita's eyes travelled to her toes. The girl had finished the pedicure and was painting her nails. She watched fascinated as they turned Deep Purple, like the rock band from her college days. She imagined that she was a bird of prey, having her talons polished and sharpened, talons that had scratched her lover's arched back, only last week, and would soon gouge into Shanti's vulnerable flesh.

They paid the parlour bill and walked to the car, which was parked nearby. It was hot; Shanti told the driver to put on air conditioning.

Shanti has her virtue and her prize-winning son, but I have her husband, thought Kavita, her hand tightening over the knife. What would happen when she told Shanti that she and Ram were lovers? Where would all that spiritual elevation and beatitude stand then? How would she see the ideal family that she had built over the years for all the world to see? Kavita felt a heady sense of power temper her misery. Maybe she could pierce that flawless heart and render it human, see Shanti cry, perhaps lash out.

She didn't know when she had first started finding Ram attractive – so well mannered, dignified, intelligent, even good looking, in a quiet way. Maybe he liked her too. She wasn't quite sure of that, but she felt he looked at her in a certain way sometimes, always looking away when she caught his gaze. When they met it was in a group, or with their partners.

After returning home from the U.S., Ram started working for his father's company. Avinash worked for his father's company as well. The two old men did business together and so did Avinash and Ram. At that time the four of them – Ram, Shanti, Kavita and Avinash – would often have dinner together. They met less after Ram started his own import-export business, a few years later. It also kept him out of town for two-three months of the year.

Then, one day, Kavita found herself in Dubai, attending the same trade fair as Ram. He suggested dinner and she agreed. At the restaurant, they talked long and intimately for the first time. Ram was so worldly, and Kavita tried to keep up. Later that night he took her hand and told her how beautiful she was, and beseeched her to come to his suite. She had resisted, but he had looked into her eyes and be-witched her. It had been quite simple really, simple and delightful.

They were free and relaxed with each other, yet there was also so much they did not know, so much to discover. When she hesitated, Ram reasoned with her, gently, always convincing her that they were do-ing no harm. Soon after coming back to Delhi, he rented an apartment in one of the city's new suburbs. Since he had always driven himself, he did not have the additional inconvenience of a driver to deal with. Kavita had managed very well too, taken aback by the ease with which she had been able to lie. This was her most mature love; one that she had no desire or power to resist. The relationship was thrilling and satisfying, holding them in its thrall even after two years.

"Won't Shanti notice all these marks!" Kavita said after their first night together.

"Don't worry. She hasn't been interested in earthly pleasures for a long time," Ram said, laughing, pull-ing her down again.

Over the years, physical affection between Kavita and Avinash had dwindled. Wasn't it supposed to be that way? They had sex very rarely, usually initiat-ed by her. Extra marital affairs were not unknown in their circle. Some of the men had mistresses and some of the wives apparently paid for the services of younger men.

As for Shanti, she had become increasingly devot-ed to her guru and his teachings. Apart from visit-ing the Centre in Delhi every week, she spent a few weekends every year attending retreats at his *ashram,* which was only a few hours' drive from the city. A group of devotees were now among her close friends. Kavita believed that she had lost the taste for sex, which had never appealed to her very much in the first place, a notion that Ram frequently reinforced.

Suddenly Kavita realized that the car wasn't going towards the Club anymore; had turned right instead of left.

"What's going on?"

"Wait and see," said Shanti with a mischievous look.

Warmth crept up Kavita's neck. No one had arranged a surprise for her in years. Avinash had organized a surprise birthday party for her once, before they got married.

Kavita straightened her back and pressed her lips firmly together. No matter, she was going to tell all today, wipe that serenity off Shanti's face, scarring her deeply and permanently.

Shanti's treat was lunch at a restaurant at the edge of the Lodi Gardens. She had asked them to cook Kavita's favourite dishes, some of which were not on the regular menu. They sat in the garden, under a white, canvas awning, while a standing fan sent gusts of warm breeze their way. Sipping a refreshing mango *lassi*, Kavita looked at the expanse of green stretching into the distance.

Turning to Shanti she said: "What's this all about? Come on, you must tell me."

"This is the 20th anniversary of the day you got engaged," Shanti said. "Do you remember?"

Kavita looked perplexed.

"It was also the day we first met. You know I keep a diary, so I am always sure of my dates. You looked so lovely, Kavita. When Avinash introduced me as Ram's wife, we were newly married ourselves then, you said – oh, then we are going to be the best of friends. I was so happy to hear that. I was new to Delhi, and very shy, and a bit lonely."

Shanti took Kavita's hand, which trembled ever so slightly, in her own.

"And it all came true, didn't it?" Shanti said.

"Did I really say that?" Kavita heard herself asking incredulously.

"Yes, you did."

Tears rose in her eyes. She blinked them back fiercely. Her hand opened and the knife fell to the hard brown earth.

Snapshot

Sukiyo feels wide awake this morning. Some mornings she wakes to a fog that haloes her mind like clouds shrouding a mountain top. Brushing her teeth, trying to rinse the taste of sour dreams from her shrunken mouth, she struggles against it. On bad days it turns into a low, persistent headache. On good days, it gradually disperses as she rolls up her *tatami* and puts it away, waters the plants and makes her first cup of tea.

Today is a good day, bright as a plum; she feels fresh and whole as she sips her warm green tea. Inhaling its familiar fragrance, she enjoys the sensation of steam rising to caress her lined face. She clears away a few grains of sugar from the dining table. Conscientious Kumiko is careless at times.

She and Kumiko, her daughter, live in an apartment in the suburbs of Tokyo. Kumiko's job is a two-hour commute, and she will be late coming home today because her company is holding its annual anniversary party.

Kumiko will have her celebration while I have mine, Sukiyo thinks, smiling.

Cup in hand, she moves to the kitchen window that overlooks the small garden. If she is early enough, she will spot Omura San, bent but strong, raking the leaves, shovelling snow, or weeding, depending on the season. Sometimes he looks up and smiles at her. If he waves, she knows he is in an exceptionally good mood. Whichever way it goes, it reassures her to catch a glimpse of him first thing in the morning.

Today the yard is empty. The snow – thick, crusty, well-packed – gleams dully under an overcast sky. It takes her back to her childhood. Walking by the blacksmith's, she would glimpse the furnace, the fire throwing the corners of the room into deep shadow. Here and there, metal emitted a cold, silvery light, like snow on a dull day. Her mother would tell her to hurry, to stop wasting time. But Sukiyo would uncharacteristically hold back, dragging her feet. This was a world she would never enter: hard, remote, masculine, smelling of horse flesh and burning coal.

There had been no snow last night. She would have known that before looking out of the window; her knee was not stiff. The arthritic knee was like a celestial *koto*, registering every whim of the weather. Today the sky was overcast, but there was one patch of brilliant blue.

"We bow respectfully twice and with deep reverence we pray. Amaterasu favours us with rain, but keeps away the wind. Today all of us unite – old and young – to pray for rain." The half-forgotten prayer unrolled in her mind like a scroll. How did it go after that?

May the black clouds over yonder mountains bring us shiny lightning and rain within limits not harmful ...

There is more, but the words have gone away. Words came and went as they pleased these days. It no longer bothered her that she had so little control over them.

Picking up a dust-cloth, she begins her chores. Usually she turns on the radio, but today she dusts in silence, her mind dwelling on the promise of the evening.

The silence that fills the tiny apartment often makes her feel heavy, like a badly made pancake. It makes her want to sit down on the faded sofa she insisted on keeping because it had come to her as a wedding gift from her aunt. The silence makes the apartment lose its proportions, making it distended and bloated, as if she were peering at it through a fish-eye lens. But today it flows like a stream along the curves of the confined space.

Wipe, polish, smooth, fold, sort, arrange: she never tires of touching things, cleaning them, putting them in order. As a child, she played outside her house in the village, in the mud, and she can still remember its smooth, wet consistency. When she was older, she squeezed goats' udders, picked fruit, combed and braided hair, kneaded dough, wove tapestries, knitted sweaters, made beds, massaged feet, prepared meals and banquets, arranged flowers. She remembers textures the way some people remember poems. Sometimes she wonders if she was meant to be born blind, but somehow escaped her destiny.

Sukiyo bows reverently before the shrine. She does this many times a day. Afterwards, she bows before the coffee table, which holds family photographs. No time to dream today, to sink into the past. A past that threatens to overwhelm her sometimes. But the pills kept it at bay.

There is so much that needs to be done to prepare for the evening. Will she manage to get everything ready before it is time for the pills and then the afternoon nap? Always that sequence – pills, nap. Pills. Nap. Never ever changing.

She turns away from the coffee table, and then turns back and picks up a picture of a pretty, unsmiling young woman in a graduation gown. Rumiko, her granddaughter, had graduated at the top of her class and was now a company vice-president. She has her own apartment in midtown Tokyo.

Sukiyo's brow creases. Rumiko is just like her photograph – efficient but cold, with an imperfectly developed heart. She replaces the photo and bows again, lower and longer this time, trying to reverse her uncharitable thoughts about Rumiko.

She must think pleasant thoughts. She has something to look forward to today. It is not going to snow. In fact, the sun will be out by noon and she will sit by the window and warm herself. Maybe she will work on the pillow cover she started to embroider months ago. She won't be able to work on it for long. Her eyes become strained easily and her hands are no longer very steady. But it is nice to open the work basket; poke around among the spools of thread, buttons, bits of cloth; look through a pattern book. Perhaps she will manage to embroider a small leaf or petal.

The pills. She goes to the kitchen and opens a drawer. There they are, laid out as usual by Kumiko. Once, she used to keep the bottles and administer the pills herself. She had been very careful, reading the labels more than once, counting the pills out properly. But that was before her illness, her long confinement in that terrible hospital. She had never lived in a hospital before, had thought she would die, not from her illness, but from being forced to be in that alien place with its manufactured normalcy. After she returned, Kumiko had taken over some of her tasks. Now she doesn't even know where the medicine bottles are kept.

If she skips the pills she will have more time. And she needs more time to prepare for the evening. She wants everything to be perfect. The mirror above the cupboard mocks her. Time? You have all the time in the world. She flicks her duster at it, as if she were shooing off a naughty child.

Such a small place this, compared to Akira's. Yet compared to Rumiko's apartment it is spacious. Akira lives in a house with a garden and a garage. There is a rose vine climbing up the side of the house and a swing at the back for the children. Kumiko has described her son's house in minute detail and they have many photographs of it.

Akira has urged his grandmother to visit him in Bangkok. He has asked her to come and spend the winter with him, promised her a wonderful vacation on the beach. He has even tried blackmail. "The children will never know you. They will grow up like orphans."

Here in the living room, Akira and his wife and two children, Kenji and Sachiko, lie within easy reach. There are three heavy photo albums devoted to Akira's household in the living-room cupboard. Two of them contain pictures of the children, from birth to the present. The third album has pictures of Akira's home and office, and of events organized by the Japan Ladies Club his wife belongs to. There are also photographs of family holidays in the States and England, Switzerland and Indonesia. She looks at one of the albums every week.

What she enjoys most is watching the video of Kenji at one. He has just perfected walking and is showing off, smiling winningly into the camera. Then he falls over a large, multicoloured beach ball. Such a clown! There is another video, a recent arrival, of his fifth birthday party, with his seven-year-old sister hovering in the background. But she prefers the earlier one.

She wants desperately to visit Akira, but she cannot. She has never left Japan. Nor does she wish to. She loves her great-grandchildren but she hates airplanes. She will never step into one.

How they droned overhead, those planes. Kumiko was just a child during the War; Sukiyo sent her away to the village. She doesn't remember anything. But she, Sukiyo, remembers everything. The planes, the bombs. Buildings crumbling, streets with gaping holes in them. People dying, dying all the time. Such pain. So much terror. Some nights she still hears screams.

The planes kept coming, tearing apart the earth and the sky. That was the worst of it, to know that they had been abandoned by Heaven. The bountiful sky, in which they read the signs of rain, thunder, snow and fair weather, had turned into a demented thing. All you could read in the sky then was death. A horrible death, without grace.

Tadeo, her husband, gone, lost to the War. Killed by a bomb that dropped out of that sky. She had been afraid to go out into an open field for years afterwards.

What is left is a snapshot. A smiling, slightly smudged Tadeo. She picks it up and runs her dust cloth over it. Next to Tadeo's picture is their wedding photograph. She is smiling uninhibitedly into the camera.

There is also a wedding album, which she has not looked at for decades. When she took it out, just once, to show it to her great granddaughter, she felt no emotion. Her life with Tadeo is too far back in time. The wedding album is like a fossil fragment buried deep in snow, somewhere.

Suddenly, she feels old. Gripping the sides of her dress, she forces herself to stand erect. Her grandmother taught her how to hold herself, how to compose her face and how to move, when she was eight or nine. "If you can control your body, your mind will follow," her grandmother used to say. She stands there remembering her grandmother, a woman as serene as the moon.

A peaceful face reflects a contented heart. A smiling face, happiness.

She thinks of Rumiko's reserved expression, and sits down on the sofa, her knees trembling.

Why was she doing this to herself? She wants to be happy today. She wants to prepare herself for the evening. She has been planning this evening for a long time; and lately, she has thought of little else.

She goes back into the kitchen and puts on a CD. Mozart, Kumiko's music. It's not bad music. It is restful, at least. She empties the plum cake mix into a pan. Not like the old days, when she cooked everything from scratch, making sure the ingredients were fresh.

Everything has become easy, and senseless. Rumiko, for instance, thinks nothing of the fact that she was sent to an expensive school and then to university. Or that she was allowed to choose the man she married. Now she has a good job that pays her a lot of money. Her husband works for an American company and lives in Seattle, wherever that is. He has been there for two years, though he went on a year's contract. He and Rumiko meet every month in Seattle or Tokyo or somewhere else. They are constantly moving, dashing here and there. Rumiko was supposed to quit her job and go to Seattle, but she has not done that. Rumiko is nearly thirty now, and childless. No one seems to care about that, or about Rumiko's odd marriage. No one but Sukiyo. But who cares what she thinks or feels?

After the cake is in the oven and the timer on, she sits down at the dining table and flips through a fashion magazine. Kumiko buys one sometimes on her way back from work. The women are all slim, young and cheerful. Usually the photographs reassure her, but somehow they have the opposite effect today.

The cake will be done any minute. They will surely like fresh baked plum cake. They won't mind that it's an instant recipe. They are in their late twenties, the girl on the phone had told her. People that age are used to synthetic things.

What if things do not go well that evening? Has she set her hopes too high?

Sukiyo moves to the window. It is snowing lightly, reminding her of fine silk, bolts and bolts of it, descending on her bed, weightless. She made two silk dresses for Kumiko's wedding trousseau. Spent days shopping for the fabric. Weeks. She'd taken immense pleasure in feeling the many textures, letting her eyes linger on the various hues and weaves until the lustre of silk had entered her soul. How happy she had been at her sewing machine!

Sukiyo enjoys looking at Kumiko's wedding albums from time to time, lingering over the close-ups. For five years after the wedding, she made trousseaux for other brides. She had not been flooded with work, but there had been enough to keep her fairly busy.

Kumiko gave birth to Akira and Rumiko, and then her husband died in a car accident. Kumiko moved in with her and found a full-time job. Sukiyo stopped tailoring to look after her grandchildren. She had not minded that. Not a bit. She had loved looking after Akira and Rumiko and doing the housework. They had been such good children. She had wanted more of her own, but life had given her only Kumiko.

She sits down by the window. If the snow continues, her knee will ache by evening. But it did not matter. She has learned to live with it. And she is glad for the company the snow provides.

The one thing that has not changed is the arrival and departure of the seasons. The autumnal trees turning winter bare and budding at the beginning of spring. The riotous blossoms and then the green intensity of summer, softened by pattering rain. The seasons must know how she waits for and watches over them.

The timer has a shrill bell. She rises hastily to turn it off. The cake has taken only twenty minutes. It is so quick, so simple, but none of these new things have melody, sweetness. They come right at you. She prefers an indirect approach. Like the way the snow, soft and white, slants towards the window. A Santoko poem drifts into her mind:

> *Brightness from the snow*
> *Fills the house with calm.*

She takes the cake out of the oven. It looks all right. The guests will enjoy it. She makes herself a large bowl of miso soup, adding tofu and pre-cooked vegetables, and eats it sitting by the window.

All too soon it is time for the pills. She didn't take them for a week once. She can't remember what happened exactly, but there had been a scene. Kumiko told her she had shouted at Rumiko, had said something nasty. What had she said? Kumiko had refused to tell her. "Surely you remember, Mother," Kumiko had said angrily.

Kumiko, who was so gentle. Always gentle Kumiko. Graceful as a swan. She had conceived her after so much difficulty, and prayer. She had brought her up well. All by herself, on her husband's pension.

Yes, she could be proud of that. If only Akira had not moved to Thailand.

Sukiyo swallows the four pills methodically, one by one.

She had not wanted to make Kumiko angry. So she had pretended that she remembered what she had said to Rumiko, and feigned regret.

Kumiko too had been a young widow. She too had chosen not to remarry. They were so alike in so many ways. Kumiko loved her, she knew that. But her daughter seldom expressed emotion; she was always so correct. Kumiko was a good daughter and mother. There was no need for uncertainty. All she should feel was pride. Pride and love.

Some people had thought that she, Sukiyo, should have helped Kumiko remarry. Well, she would not have objected if Kumiko had brought a decent young man home. But she never had. Perhaps Kumiko was too refined to marry again. Sukiyo had never once considered that possibility for herself, though there had been hints and suggestions of offers. She was sure Kumiko felt the same way.

Sukiyo takes off her dress and removes her slippers. Slipping into a nightgown, she gets into bed and opens the drawer of the bedside table. As always, she takes out a photo of chubby baby Kenji. There she is, holding him in her arms, before he went to live so far away. She'd made low, cooing sounds and he had looked intently at her, with alert, shining eyes. Through the folds of the thin blanket, Sukiyo had felt his incredible softness and warmth. She'd bent her head down, inhaling his sweet baby smell. Akira was the spitting image of her husband. And Kenji in turn looked like his father.

She puts the photograph away, smiling. She is superstitious about it; she believes that a glimpse will ensure untroubled sleep.

Two hours later, she wakes and switches off the musical alarm clock. She gets up and goes to the bathroom, and pats her face with a cool, damp towel. Then she goes back into the bedroom and opens her wardrobe. Pushing aside the dresses, skirts and blouses, she looks at the delicately patterned kimono, which hangs at the very end. Her other kimonos are packed away, but she has kept this one, a little guiltily, knowing that the silk would be better preserved if it was stored properly. She longs to wear it on this very special evening. But it is too ostentatious. She does not want to cross the line of propriety.

She strokes the kimono and then lets it fall back into the darkness. The plain but elegant blue skirt and the white blouse with the frilly collar and cuffs is more appropriate. She pulls the clothes on slowly, ritualistically. She hasn't got dressed up in a while. It makes her feel younger. In control. She brushes her hair and puts it up in a simple knot. Then she scrutinizes herself in the mirror. Satisfied, she steps into the living room. It is as she left it, neat as a pin. Next she inspects the kitchen. Perfect.

Everything was going to go well, she is certain of that now. She has had a sign – a dream about the Taasobi fertility rite.

In the dream, she was back in the village. An old man was dancing to the thumping of a huge drum. Using a twig decorated with a rice ball, he mimicked the act of tilling the soil. Someone in the crowd had raised her voice to the sky, chanting:

> *This is the rice nursery of the Great Celestial Luminous God.*

Oh Daimyo, oh wives, children, tillers of the fields, let us all joyfully sow!

Wild drumbeats and exuberant dancing; everyone, men, women, children, caught in a frenzy of living. She cannot remember all of the dream, but this fragment is enough. It is precious.

The doorbell rings at the appointed hour. She opens the door to a smiling young couple with a baby. She asks the man and the woman to come in and sit down. There is a round of introductions. The young man pays her a compliment about her appearance. The woman compliments her house. "How beautifully kept it is! And the furnishings, they are so tasteful." Sukiyo smiles and talks about Kumiko. She points out the neatly arranged photographs.

"How beautiful the children are! Where are they now?" asks the woman. Sukiyo tells her, but she is getting anxious.

The baby is quiet, inert, in the woman's arms, all wrapped up in blankets. It is a real baby, isn't it? Or is it a doll? One could never tell these days. But the girl on the phone had promised a real baby.

Sukiyo had spotted the ad right away in the newspaper, even though it had been a small one, buried on a back page. "Do you miss the touch of a child's hand on your cheek? Are your relatives too far away or too busy to visit you? We offer you a real family ..." She had put the paper away, offended at the bluntness of the ad.

Then one day she had impulsively dialled the number. A very nice receptionist had explained everything to her, telling her again and again how easy it was, how pleasant and affordable. She could use a credit card. All they needed was the number. Kumiko had given Sukiyo a credit card that she used when

Kumiko took her shopping. She asked the woman to wait while she got her purse, and then she read the number to her over the phone. Her heart had beaten like the drum in the dream.

And now they are here with the baby. Such a nice couple too. The young man has such charming manners, quite old fashioned.

Sukiyo goes to the kitchen to prepare tea. The young woman offers to help, and hands the baby to the man. The baby stirs, rubbing its nose with its little fist.

"I think he's going to wake up now," the young woman says.

"May I hold him?" Sukiyo asks. A quick look passes between the man and the woman. Perhaps it is against company policy to handle the baby? She feels her spirits drop like a felled kite.

"Of course," says the man. He places the baby gently in her arms. Yes, it was beginning to wake up – yawning, rubbing its face, frowning. She turns to the man and says, with complete confidence, "There's a camera, right behind you, in the top drawer of that cupboard. Could you take a photograph, please?"

She looks at the baby. Its eyes are open and it is staring at her, unblinking. She feels the gaze, intense and pure, cut through to her heart, cleansing it of all doubt.

"He's normally restless with new people, but he really likes you," the woman says. "How quietly he's lying in your arms!"

Sukiyo looks up at the camera and smiles a full, uninhibited smile, as the flash goes off.

Reveries of a Riot

The riot has raged outside Mira's window for two days. The window is large and square. Lacy, white curtains frame it on the inside. A second set of curtains, in rough-textured *khadi*, patterned with maroon and green stripes, protects the lace from the searing heat of the sun. They keep out the glare on reclining Sunday afternoons, when Mira reads, dozes, embroiders or listens to Hindustani classical music as the lazy softness of a stretching cat steals over her.

The window has remained shut. So has their front door. They haven't stirred out while the curfew flickers on and off outside, like a light bulb gone crazy. Mira is nearly out of fresh milk and running low on vegetables.

During this time of enforced rest, Mira returns to the window again and again. She sits at some distance from it, curled up on the overstuffed sofa, or straight up in the old, rocking chair. Or down on the carpet, knees drawn to her chin, to contemplate the window. The window has become not something to look out of, but something to look at.

On the first day of the riot, Mira, and her husband Nimish, were getting ready to go to work, when they heard shouts, the sound of running feet, breaking glass and then a gunshot. They rushed to the window. Nimish put out a hand to prevent Mira from sticking her head out too far. All they saw at first were three men running away, and broken glass on the pavement opposite their apartment building. Either the tailoring shop or the bakery, or both, must have been vandalized.

Mira felt Nimish draw in his breath sharply. It was then that she saw the body, sprawled face down on the pavement.

Mira's first commonplace thought was: this is like the movies. She expected to see a thin trickle of blood run out from under the man's feet into the open drain, turning the brown sewage water to a darker hue.

But there was no blood that day, or the next, just distant shouts and screams.

The next morning, the contents of the tailoring shop and the bakery – shelves and counters, trays and sewing machines, chairs and curtains, knick knacks – had been dented or broken, and thrown on the pavement. Some of the things had spilled onto the street.

The attack must have occurred at dawn, before they had woken up and taken positions beside the window. They had missed the action. They had heard more than they had seen, their view confined to the narrow strip of road, pavement and house fronts framed by their window, while their ears extended like antenna, picking up distorted air waves from all around.

On the first day, they had felt compelled to spend long hours at the window, to monitor the riot on the radio and the television (which weren't giving much away). And on the telephone. It was a day punctuated by quick visits from the neighbours – speculative conversations, forced little jokes, lamentations on the state of the government, politics, the country and the world, hastily exchanged reassurances.

They had said, over and over, among themselves, that things could not go on like this. Tempers had to cool. People would come back to their senses.

The anger and hate would be snuffed out by death, the smell of death filling the streets and the houses, spreading over the city like an oil spill contaminating the sea. The anger and hate would be diluted by the wailing of frightened children, the ritualized mourning of widows, the public grief of relatives — loud, harsh, unrelenting.

There was the police force, and the army. The army would know how to handle a situation like this, even if the police failed. Community groups too would play a role, surely, going door to door, counselling, consoling, pleading, haranguing.

Peace would come. It might take some time, but it would descend, eventually, like a soothing late-monsoon shower, gentle and fragrant.

Meanwhile it was best to stay indoors. Stay calm, in control. Do ordinary, everyday things — cooking, eating, sleeping — that would blanket the insanity that had taken over the streets. And keep thoughts from scattering in unseemly directions.

On that near-normal, first day of the riot, Mira walked around their spacious living room, over furnished at the edges, examining the many things — inherited, gifted, bought, picked up, and others that seemed to have turned up on their own — with a solemn interest.

She spent quite a while at the bookshelves, specially the one that held the old, mouldy books that smelt so good. Here were the world classics, *Wuthering Heights* nestling next to *War and Peace*, *The Trial* cheek-to-jowl with *The Old Man and the Sea*.

And the books on Hindu spirituality — the *Upanishads*, the *Bhagwat Geeta*, the writings of Ramkrishna Paramhans, Swami Vivekanand, Shri Aurobindo and

the Mother. These books had belonged to Mira's fa-
ther-in-law, whom she had never met. He had passed
away when Nimish was just 10 years old.

A newer and smaller bookshelf was devoted to
Graham Greene, Gabriel Garcia Marquez, Italo Calvino,
Toni Morrison, Salman Rushdie, Bapsi Sidhwa, Amitav
Ghosh, and others. The two remaining bookshelves could
have been labelled "his" and "hers." One held Nimish's
books on engineering, management and cricket, plus a
smattering of poetry, in English and Gujarati.

Mira's bookshelf contained scholarly volumes on
sociology. She had started the collection when she
had embarked on her Masters of Social Work at the
Tata Institute of Social Sciences, and had meticulous-
ly added to it through the six subsequent years of her
professional life in academia.

Here you could also find cookery books – the re-
gional cuisine from the many Indian states – and pattern books on embroidery, books on feminism, and
old magazines – *Eve's Weekly*, in its more radical avatar, *Manushi*, *Filmfare*, and the *Economic and Political
Weekly*; half a dozen Hindi novels and a few volumes
of *Abhilasha*, a Hindi literary quarterly.

There was so much that they had brought with
them when they had got married and so much more
they had acquired through the five years that followed – coffee tables, wooden screens, flower vas-
es, painted pottery, terracotta ashtrays, handicrafts,
clocks, photographs, records and cassettes, letters...

Mira had enjoyed yelling through the bedroom
door at Nimish: do-you-remember-such-and-such-
thing-event-person? Nimish had come into the
drawing room for a while, and they had laughingly
recalled the histories and biographies of the various
objects, till Nimish, tiring of the game, had retired
to the bedroom with the latest issue of *Business India*,

and Mira had fallen once again into a silent contemplation of the window.

On the second day of the riot, there were no visits from the neighbours, or phone calls from friends, as though the event had gone from being a collective tragedy to a personal failure that had to be dealt with in harrowing aloneness, sealed indoors, exiled into the self.

On the second day, Nimish stayed in the bedroom, Mira in the living room. The violent fight they had had the night before drove them to carve out their separate spheres and stay within their isolated, but still-connected spaces.

There hadn't been very much else to do but look at the window. Its perfect symmetry. The white casement slightly scratched and chipped in places. The curtains half drawn back. The play of light against delicate lace. The panes, dusty but secure. Whole, when there were so many shattered windows on their street, in their city. So much glittering, crunchy glass everywhere.

Whole. What a wonderful word. Treacherous though. Watch out for that one. Take away the "w" and a gaping wound opens. An external wound you think at first. Superficial. Easily healed. But a second look reveals that the knife has cut through the layers of skin to reach the vital organs, now a bloody, implacable mess, threatening to break through to the surface to reveal the hopelessness of the affliction.

What a wonderful, whole window. Watching it was both delight and torment. Wanting it to stay intact. Wanting it to shatter. Who were the lucky ones? Who had got it right? Those whose windows had been broken, or those who had found refuge behind their unblemished windows?

It was the eve of Holi, the night when Holika, the demoness, one of Prahlad's tormentors, sits on a burning pyre with Prahlad in her lap. She is protected by a special shawl, but Lord Vishnu saves Prahlad, his devotee, and consigns Holika to the flames. It was on the eve of Holi that Mira was entranced by a bonfire, once, a long time ago.

The colony boys had built a huge bonfire in the field, in front of Mira's house. Mira had watched them building it all evening, knowing that something significant was to come, but without a clue to what it might be.

The bonfire had been set alight after it got dark, by the light of lanterns, exciting, shadowy things in themselves. A roaring fire took birth with everyone milling around it, singing, dancing and eating sweets.

Mira did not join the festivities. She sat on the grass – a chubby girl with glasses – watching the flames rise and lick the sky, turning her world into a blaze, while the piercing heat turned her insides rosy warm and liquid. Later, her mother had half dragged half carried her home.

Still Mira watched the flames from her bedroom window, her mind blank, the fire consuming her from inside out, making her whole.

She had fallen asleep at her vigil, by the window, and woken up early as the first light of the day had crept into her eyes, through shuttered eyelids.

As soon as her eyes opened Mira looked out of the window expecting to see the fire, which was gone. Mira's heart started to beat hard. She rushed out of the house in her rubber slippers and pyjamas, knowing her mother would scold her if she found out, and ran, panting, half-falling, feeling a little sick, to the spot where the bonfire had been.

A perfect circle of ash, charred twigs and burnt grass stood in the field. As Mira walked into it, the acrid smell filled her to choking and crumbling ashes, powdery soft and still warm, tickled the edges of her feet.

Looking up, Mira saw the arching blue sky go from pink to gold. It was immense, whole, like the fire had been. Bending down she grabbed fistfuls of ash. She had preserved that ash in a toffee tin for many years after that.

The fascination with the window was less innocent. But there was no option: the entrancement had to run its course.

Blood. It would have been nice to see some. Snarling red, viscous. Bubbling as if in anger. Simmering as if full of spite. What use a riot or a fight without the redness, the richness of real blood?

It would have been good to see a stone, stones, strike the windowpanes. Enter the living room and fall with a reverberating thud that shook the somnolent apartment.

It would have been good to see the glass crack, the pane turn into an intricate spider's web, while the other shattered and fell to the floor, tinkling.

Shards of glass everywhere. Glass, pure and beautiful. What use a riot or a fight without broken glass, without the hardness, the sharpness, the clarity of glass?

But there had been no blood.

There had never, it seemed, been any *real* blood in Mira's life, unless one counted tame, menstrual blood, stale and sour smelling. More real to her than her own blood was the tomato-ketchup blood of the countless Hindi movies that Mira had grown up on.

At first the blood spilled on screen appeared to have a good reason to be there. It was spilled in the name of righteousness, honour, justice, love, filial devotion. But as the years rolled on, the bloodbaths got more and more senseless, random and gory. The films were holding up mirrors to the reality around them.

Mira and her friends started seeing these movies less and less as time passed, because they seemed to have nothing to do with *their ideas, their motivations, their lives*. The movies had created their own universe and occupied an orbit that did not overlap with the space that defined Mira's life.

But as the first day of the riot had started to fade into night, Mira had felt her blood coursing through her veins once again, after a long time indeed. She had experienced it as a warm, living thing, intent on action.

She couldn't figure out what had triggered off this unfreezing of her blood, and her spirit, which had brought on the desperate urge to let her innards spill out through her mouth, her sole weapon.

Words had spewed out of Mira with a damning ferocity that night, when everything had seemed under control, in the beginning. All that time she had believed that the violence outside was an external event, unreal and transient. It had nothing to do with *her, with Nimish — their ideas, their motivations, their lives.*

They would move, Nimish had said. They lived in a predominantly Muslim neighbourhood, in the poorer part of Bombay, because they had been unable to find anything else. They had been searching for a flat for over six months. They had been too picky. That's why they hadn't found anything yet. They had to be realistic. They had to compromise. They would settle for a half way decent place in a nice locality. They would leave here as soon as they could.

"And what about us? Do you think that we will solve any of that by moving?"

"Don't start on that now, Mira. Not tonight of all nights. Please." Flames licked at the corners of Mira's mind. Flames and fire, so central to Indian life, and death – the ancient fascination that still endures.

Sacred fire, ultimate purifier, made profane by *sati* and bride burning. The rites and wrongs of fire still endure.

The body is consumed by fire to be made whole. Fire unlocks the spirit, which merges with the whole. Fire is not so much death, as it is purification and after-life. So self immolation still endures – suicide and self-expression, an end and a new beginning, rolled eerily into one.

The rioters had overturned three buses and set them ablaze, on the main road not far from where Mira lived. That must have been some bonfire!

Flames licked at the corners of Mira's mind, and she blazed with words.

Afterwards, after her eruption into angry utterances and Nimish's wordy counter attack, Mira felt empty and slack, de-muscled, limpid.

It was as if a great wind had blown through their flat, whirled all the objects around, shaken them up and set them back in their place, cleansed.

She felt she did not need to talk to Nimish ever again. This had been her first real conversation with him. And it had explained their life together with the geometric precision of the circle of ash left behind by the Great Bonfire.

As a child Mira had seen practically no anger or violence in her home. Her parents seemed always calm, though her father seemed a little sad at times and her mother would get somewhat testy. There appeared to be no quarrels or disagreements between them. Perhaps they had chosen consciously to turn away from overt expression.

Things did not change very much in her adult life, which seemed, more or less like a seamless continuation of her tranquil childhood.

Before Mira and Nimish had found this flat, they had lived for a couple of months in a friend's apartment, where they had had to suffer a violent neighbour.

Shouts and screams, the sounds of banging doors and falling things, whimpers and sobs, emanated at odd hours from the neighbouring apartment. Perhaps they hadn't been all that loud, but in the hushed silence of her temporary home, which had echoed the hollow quiet of her parents' house, the sounds had the impact of gunshots fired at a distance. Mira remembered thinking that someday, perhaps, the bullets would pierce the walls of her own home.

Standing at their window Mira would see the man storm out of the apartment building after a virulent sounding quarrel, get into the car and drive away noisily, leaving behind a swirl of dust. Sometimes, though less often, the woman would walk out of the house, a little unsteady, her *pallu* wrapped tightly around her head, dragging a sobbing child with her, to hail a rickshaw as it rounded a corner and disappear.

Through all this Nimish assured Mira, again and again, that they would move soon. They were spending all their after-work hours looking for a house; they were bound to find something. He appeared to get used to the situation but Mira couldn't stop herself from listening and looking out for their neighbours all the time.

She started leading a double life, lurking, in her mind, through the rooms of her neighbour's house, a ghost haunted by an intense and unnatural curiosity, even as she sat down to dinner with Nimish, or brought out her embroidery books in the drawing room or watched her husband wrestle with the Rubik's cube.

That was the feeling she experienced once again, as the riot raged outside their window. As she sat in her cozy, little home, leafing through glossy magazines, she was a ghost slipping through the restless streets.

Now she was part of the crowd that jeered and cheered, hurled stones and abuse and set things alight. (What delight in seeing the flames rise high and lick the sky!) The crowd that had become a single moving, tensing, preying beast, intent on action …

Now she was at a dingy, way-side, tea stall, listening to the rabble-rouser at the upturned table, his speech and spittle darting back and forth between him and his audience, people listening, forgetting their companions, the tea turning tepid in their cups, Someone whistled. Someone clapped. "Kya hero aadmi hai." What a heroic man.

Then she was moving down a street where everything was burning, the houses, the shops, the cars, the people, and she was dodging falling rafters and flying sparks, walking around the blazing bodies rolling on the ground, trying to quell the flames, hanging on to life in the throes of death, she was shrinking from burning limbs that were thrust at her from writhing heaps. And everywhere the stench of burning flesh …

She was on a street now where there were no people and no fires, only glass, everywhere, crushed glass covering the sidewalk and road and the walls of buildings, the whole world so crystalline and beautiful, blinding her with its brilliance …

Then she was on her own street, which had been all cleaned up. There were people going about their business, unsmiling, silent.

Mira walked along quickly, uneasily down the street and towards her house, knowing that if someone made one small, false move the façade of normalcy would crumble and there would be glass on the street and the sound of running feet and shouts and gunshots.

They all had to be very, very careful. She knew that with an absolute certainty that made her break out in sweat. What if it was she who did something wrong?

She felt a scream forming at the base of her throat and rising slowly, and then she was at the entrance of her building, her self control deserting her as soon as she was inside the door, making her run up the hollow-sounding, wooden staircase, till she collided into a man who was going down the stairs.

As she brushed against him Mira got a whiff of his sweat mingled with that other body smell, unmistakable despite her fear and the darkness that enveloped the staircase. This man was her first lover, who had been at one time as big as the bonfire, in Mira's life, blotting out everything else.

He seemed to recognize her and paused, though he had been in a great hurry a second ago. For a moment they withdrew into themselves, preparing for the encounter. Then they embraced.

Tongues of fire licked at Mira's skin. Her body felt translucent, cool, like fine glass. He kissed her roughly on her mouth. He had a week-old beard that scratched her face. He hadn't had the time to shave or hadn't bothered to. He seemed agitated, his body too warm, trembly. Mira clung closer to him and pushed her tongue into his feverish mouth.

He had been there, out on the streets, rioting. His clothes and skin were street-stained. Nothing else could explain his disturbed state.

Perhaps, at first, he had just been a passerby, on a mindless errand, walking hurriedly down a street. Perhaps he had left his quiet side-street and walked onto a main street, into the eye of an inferno, surrounded suddenly by a throng of angry, shouting, crazed people throwing stones and hitting out at whatever they could find. Being of an excitable nature, the impressionistic young man that he was, perhaps he had been drawn in by the crowd, a participant rather than spectator in the random violence that created its purpose as it went along.

As Mira slipped her hand into his she felt the grainy texture of mud on them.

The images of the streets outside coalesced into a single flame and burned in Mira's mind. She felt as if he shared the flame. That, in fact, he was fuelling and brightening it as his body heat seeped into her. As they kissed, breathing chaotically, Mira pushed hard against him, wanting the street-sweat, mud-violence; the feverish hunger-anger of his tongue to infuse her being as well.

He led Mira by hand to the top of the building, to the little recess, musty, cobwebbed, stacked with discarded junk that led to the terrace, which was locked.

Half undressing, they clung, clawed, bit, thrust, tugged, stroked each other, in a frenzy of love and despair. As he took her standing up, Mira felt his calloused hands (what had he been doing with his butter-smooth hands, soft and gentle in her memory?) grasp her hair, gather it in his fist, and pull her head back, hard. Pain, black and deep, washed over her as she came and came.

Now she was no longer apart, but a part of the riot, and would always be, with a part of the riot inside her forever.

He left her outside her flat. A brush of lips against her earlobe, a hand momentarily tightening around hers and he faded away. She couldn't smell him any longer. Though she could feel him still. Mira stood in the dark for a while, running her fingers over her swollen lips. Then she let herself into the apartment.

They had picked the body off the pavement that very day, the first day of the riot. Late in the afternoon an ambulance had driven up, a siren rending the air. Two policemen had got out of the van and hauled the corpse into the car. There was no blood on the man's clothes. It was not anyone they could recognize, no one they had seen before in the neighbourhood.

There were no marks on the pavement, at least nothing they could see at that distance.

Mira could picture the body lying on the cold bunk inside the ambulance, which must smell depressingly of disinfectant. Surely they would cover it with a sheet. What a strange corpse! The Hindus covered their dead from neck to toe in a white sheet, and bedecked them in garlands of flowers. The exposed faces were set in repose. They lay on *charpoys* held aloft by four or five men, dressed in white, freshly bathed, who carried the corpse down the street chanting "*Ram naam satya hai.*" *The name of God is True.* The Muslim corpses were also white-clad, and placed inside plain coffins. The bearers remained silent sometimes, at times chanting, "*La-ilaaha-illallah.*" *There is no deity but God.* The Hindus were destined for a funeral pyre, the Muslims for a grave. Either way, they were dead, cold, gone.

The man had been felled by a single bullet. They had heard just one shot. Who knows whom the bullet had been meant for? Who knows how many sightless, meandering bullets had been forced to find a kill – someone who happened to be at a window, someone going about on a mundane errand, someone who had tried to duck into a doorway, some idiot with his back to the wall?

It's getting dark outside so Mira goes into the kitchen to cook some *dal-chawal*. She decides to use the two remaining onions for the *dal*. Pulling out the knife, she goes chop-chop-chop. The blade slices rhythmically through the skin to reach the heart and goes on to the other side. Soon there is a heap of finely chopped onion on the board. Tears run down

Mira's face and she wipes them inadequately with her sleeve.

Her untended shrine with its wilting flowers catches her eye. It's a narrow shelf crammed with Hindu gods. Laxmi, Vishnu, Ganesh, Shiva, Krishna, Durga – they are all there. She is not a believer; performing the *puja* every morning is a gesture she makes for her mother-in-law who gave her these family idols. Every evening a boy delivers the customary packet of fresh flowers at her doorstep, one of the ritual *puja* offerings. Yesterday of course he had not come.

"Allah ho Akbar." God is great. Mira watches Nimish through the kitchen door as he starts up on hearing the familiar prayer call. They haven't heard it for two days. His eyes meet hers and turn hastily away.

There's a knock on the door. The neighbours start dropping in, in quick succession. There has been no curfew today, the third day of the riot. And if the mosque has been opened again, then everything must be all right.

I can go to work tomorrow, thank god, says one neighbour, I have to finish this important report for these clients who are coming in next week. They're Japanese, you know.

Mira brews cups of tea and hands them out through the kitchen door to Nimish, leaving him to deal with the visitors. She hates him for expressing different views to different neighbours, depending on their religion.

Tomorrow she would walk down the street, going around the area where the dead man had lain, superstitious and queasy about stepping into that space, but unable to shake off a horrible curiosity that would lead her to closely examine the ground as she went by.

The bakery and the tailor shop would be repaired. The week after she would go into the bakery to buy savoury *naan* bread to go with the *kheema-muttar* that she makes so well.

Later, she would go into the tailor shop with her magenta-silk blouse piece, to have a blouse stitched in the latest style, where the tailor's wife, her *burqa* thrown back over her broad, impassive face, would hand her dog-eared pattern books from under the counter.

Wearing the new blouse, her gorgeous, new *Kanjivaram* sari rippling and crackling around her, she would go, a week later, to her cousin's wedding, where they would not discuss the riot. The talk would centre on the decorations, the excess or simplicity of the jewellery on the women guests, the groom's income, the bride's beauty and the quality of the ice cream served at the reception.

How would she conduct herself with the baker and the tailor, her neighbours, after all, if only by chance? Would she smile effusively at them, while they, addressing her as "*behenji*," sister, ask after Nimish *miya's* health? Or would their transactions be concluded in an aura of bewildering guilt and shame, with an absence of eye contact and a minimum of conversation?

Suddenly Mira decides that she has to get out of the apartment. Opening her closet, she finds a *dupatta* and drapes it around her head. She takes off her *bindi* and sticks it on the mirror of the dressing table. Telling Nimish that she is going out for a while, she sweeps past him and out of the door before he has time to react.

Mira goes unhurriedly down the stairs and into the semi-deserted streets. They are somewhat cleaner than she had expected, though there is more than the usual load of garbage piled up at street corners. The streets are surprisingly devoid of policemen. Here and there are burnt out shells of things that were formerly whole.

Almost all the shops are closed, and there's a plethora of them – small, individualistic shops selling fabric, clothes, shoes, toys, school goods, *attar* and incense, jewellery, buttons and lace, kitchenware, hardware, food, dairy products. There are shops that repair watches, leather goods, bicycles. A couple of the groceries have their doors half open.

The neighbourhood is old, the majority of the buildings dilapidated, badly in need of a coat of paint. They contrast sharply with the occasional, smart, new apartment building, which is architecturally stark and angular. The older buildings have graceful, curved balconies, with wrought-iron railings and their windows and doors, composed of softly rotting wood, are framed by patterned arches, the designs either floral or geometric or a combination, looking as if they have half melted into the ancient façades.

Mira gets off the bigger and wider road and goes down a familiar *gulli*, twisted and aromatic, past children playing hopscotch and skipping rope. A little girl in heavy pigtails catches her eye and smiles shyly.

She pauses as she finds herself approaching the mosque. The door is ajar. Prayers spill out of the courtyard into the dusky air. The minarets are outlined as inspiring silhouettes against the clear, blue sky.

Mira goes up to the door and peeps in. Inside there are a dozen men in white *kurta-pajamas*, and knitted skull caps, kneeling, bent over so that their heads almost touch the floor, praying. They are all grouped together at the far corner of the courtyard.

The openness of the courtyard comes as a shock after the circumscribed space of the apartment. Mira feels exhilarated. As she watches, the space seems to hum, extend outwards and upwards.

In the centre of the courtyard is a group of pigeons, hopping and fluttering. The soft, grey bodies cut a pleasing pattern against the beautiful, marble floor.

The pigeons take off and within seconds they are afloat, high in the sky, flying in formation. Mira watches them till they disappear, mingling smokily in the blue-grey sky.

Suddenly she is melancholy. How limiting it was to be outside the mosque! Excluded also from the flight of the pigeons, with only the option of a linear escape – the shutting of windows and the slamming of doors?

Mira slowly makes her way back home.

Kathmandu

April woke to the insistent buzzing of a fly. It took her a moment to remember where she was. Her eyes automatically followed the fly's erratic path from the edge of her ear, to the slope of the pillow, till it dropped out of sight.

Turning slowly, she lay on her back, looking up at the white ceiling with yellowing patches on it, probably created by moisture. They are good at getting water to come out of the ceiling, but not the tap, she thought. Right away she felt ashamed. How bitchy! It was horrible. She was not like that.

The fly had reappeared. Like an inspired lover, this time it tried to get into her ear. She waved it away dispiritedly. The flies, mosquitoes and other insects did not bother her that much any more. It was futile to fight them. One just had to endure. That's what her older sister, Joyce, had said to her on the phone the other day.

April pictured Joyce in her trendy, Toronto apartment, cell phone in one hand, cigarette in the other, looking out at Lake Ontario – vast, placid and soothing. A slim shoreline and an endless stretch of water, under a spreading sky. Empty space. There was none of that in Thamel, the touristy neighbourhood in Kathmandu where she had landed.

The buildings were chock-a-block, grungy, the streets crooked, the pavements non-existent, or broken down and taken over by people selling all sorts of stuff. The buildings here were not very tall, but they chopped off the sky all the same, pushing out real air, allowing motorcycle exhaust to linger.

"Isn't it something?" Kevin had said, when the taxi brought them from the simple little airport, through the relatively spacious suburbs, into the density of Thamel. "All these people and things and colours?" He had turned towards April, his eyes spritely.

April, numbed by the flights, had nodded, feeling her heart sink a little at the oppressiveness of the scene, its squalor and … And what? She didn't really have words for it. There were only feelings, unpleasant ones.

I'll be fine tomorrow, after I've slept, she told herself.

At the shabby, little hotel, two Nepali men – short, uniformed and smiling – had helped them drag their massive backpacks up three flights of narrow, uneven stairs, to a dingy room.

Even the air felt different, and the "natural spring water" they drank from large, plastic bottles had a weird taste. Even that. This was what surprised her. She had expected everything to be different but not air, not water. Despite the strangeness of it all, April had fallen asleep right away.

She turned her face towards the window, with its rusting, horizontal, iron bars; its lower half covered by a faded, flower-patterned curtain. Beyond the bars she could see a fragment of sky, the branches of a mango tree – she had been told that's what it was – and part of a satellite dish.

How April had pleaded with her father to finance the trip; and got Joyce to put in a word on her behalf.

But why do you want to go there, her father had asked. It's dangerous. They're in the middle of a civil war; you know that, don't you? You could get cholera. Malaria. Why don't you go somewhere else? How about Greece, or the Caribbean?

To his questions April provided no answers, though she assured him that she would take all the vaccines and follow the advice given by the travel clinic to the T. Joyce knew why she was going; she was following Kevin.

That Kevin, Joyce had said. I know the type. Best to work him out of your system. April had been stung, but had said nothing. Her sister was a sharp-tongued cynic, but she was also generous and caring.

Her father had finally relented and she had said a round of goodbyes to her school friends in Burlington. The plan had blown them away. She had pretended to be cool. Yes she was going to travel in Asia for three months, skipping the fall term during her second year at the University of Toronto. It was not such a big deal. Really.

April looked at her little black alarm clock, which sat on the bedside table. It was 10:30. The time for breakfast had passed. She had missed it again. Not that she cared. There was a bag of chips and a banana somewhere. She would get up, dress, and carry these up to the terrace. Or she could go next door and get a papaya milkshake.

She loved the terrace that allowed her to look down on the streets, the shops and the people, without being seen. More importantly, she could look up at the sky and breathe. Yesterday, when the clouds had lifted, she had clearly seen the mountains in the distance. The faint outline, just the hint of a range, presented itself, triangular wedges that thrust upwards gloriously, their tops crowned by pale silver snow. A thrill ran through her. For a few moments she floated free of her ailing body, her unquiet stomach and her hazy head.

On their first day, she had felt a bit suffocated in their small hotel room. When she had said that they should perhaps pay a little more for a bigger one, Kevin had suggested that she go check out the terrace.

How had he known about the terrace, she wondered. She would have never suspected that it was there – a terrace right at the top of the building, on its roof, with a solid, waist-high wall.

Kevin had been at home in Kathmandu as soon as they got off the plane, even though this was his first time here. He was an experienced traveller; he had taught English in Thailand and worked on an organic farm in South Africa. That had been part of his charm.

April decided that she would go downstairs after all. She had spent the day before in bed, except for that half an hour before sunset, on the terrace. After dinner in the room, sticking to sandwiches, she had gone downstairs and watched TV.

In the common room were a young Nepali man and a little boy, their eyes glued to the set. It was some American station, not one that she knew well. She had taken in images of skyscrapers, fireplaces, skiers photographed from dramatic angles, teens with extravagant hair executing thrilling turns on rollerblades, women in smart business suits that revealed sleek, stockinged knees, close-ups of succulent steaks, the melting innards of chocolate cookies – the world she had left behind.

She had marvelled at the speed – all the swish, whoosh, zip and zoom – on that small screen, in that low-lit, yellowish room, with old furniture. She could see the darkness pressing against the half curtained window. That was another thing. The dark here was different too, thicker, stickier. It reminded her of the weird, black, gelatinous something she had eaten once, at a Bubble Tea café in Toronto.

She hadn't stayed downstairs long, coming back to the room and listening to music on her Discman, before falling asleep.

Getting out of bed, April washed up, and put on a light dress. She would have liked a shower, but she had to switch on a little heater and leave it on for 10 minutes to get hot water, something that she found hard to remember. The banana on the dresser looked black and squishy, and gave off a strong smell. She dropped it in the wastebasket. Taking her bag and hat, April walked downstairs.

A waiter made his way towards her as she was crossing the dining room, "Breakfast?" he queried with a smile.

"But I am too late."

"No problem. Fried eggs. Scrambled. Omelette on toast. Juice. Coffee."

April let herself be led to a table, next to a large, potted plant. She was going to eat all that and more.

"Cornflakes?" she asked as she sat down.

The waiter took her order and shuffled off. She noticed that he was quite old, 60ish probably, though she found it hard to tell people's age here. It was a bit like when she went to Chinatown in Toronto.

Chinatown had fascinated her when she first moved to Toronto from Burlington. She used to go into the grocery shops to look at all the strange bottles and tins, and read the badly translated labels. The exotic fruits were a particular attraction – lychee, jackfruit, persimmon. But she had never got around to buying anything, though she and her housemates often did cheap, Chinese take-out from a place near their apartment.

As she settled back in her chair, April realized that she and Kevin had sat at the same table for breakfast on the first day.

Kevin's face had loomed over hers, too large, too white. "I'll just be gone for three days," it had said. "Four at most. You'll be much better by then and we can really start planning what we want to do."

That was the last she had seen of him, as she lay in bed, having just taken the medicine that he had brought her. He was telling her that he wanted to go white water rafting, but only if it was okay with her.

She had lain there, looking at him, trying to figure out what he was saying.

"And Pat will be here. I'll tell her to look in on you. Plus the people at this hotel are super helpful. I know you feel awful, but it'll be okay. It's always like this in the beginning. Doesn't last long. A few days rest and you'll be fine."

April watched Kevin packing, wordlessly, through half-closed eyes, her eyelids getting heavier, till she fell into a feverish doze. Later, surfacing momentarily, she felt Kevin's lips brush against her hair. Then he was gone.

She was furious the next day, furious and grievously hurt, when she fully grasped what he had done. She had tried to call her best friend, Ann-Marie, in Burlington, but had not got through. So she had called Joyce, who had given her the unlikely advice about enduring. Kevin had texted her at mid-day, saying that he hoped she was better, and that he would likely be out of range for the next 48 hours. She had ignored the message. He hadn't even had the decency to call. He was a creep, and a cheap one at that.

April finished her breakfast, washing it all down with a vanilla milkshake. Unfortunately their hotel did not do papaya. It was amazing how her appetite had revived; she had eaten very little yesterday. She rose and walked into the little walled courtyard at the back of the hotel, which was her second favourite place, after the terrace.

Pat was sitting there, under the shade of a large, leafy tree, reading. One of her feet rested on a little stool, displaying an ankle encased in a plaster cast. A thick staff that she used to propel herself around was propped up against a nearby chair.

She looked up from her book and smiled at April. "How are you feeling?" she asked in a cheerful tone.

"Better," April said.

"Sit," she said, pointing to an empty chair beside her. "I was wondering when you would emerge."

Pat looked right at her. Her eyes were light blue, with little wrinkles around them. April found her direct gaze a bit disconcerting, but she did not look away. She must be in her mid-60s, April decided. Most of her short, brown hair had turned white. Neither of them spoke for a minute.

Then Pat said: "Nice day, isn't it?"

Sunny, dry, 22 degrees centigrade, April would've guessed.

"Yes," she said.

"Do you like sun or rain?" Pat asked.

April was not sure what to say.

"Or should one say sun or snow?" Pat said with a smile.

"Both," said April. "I like a sunny day with snow on the ground."

"That's nice," said Pat. "Canada, I never did get out there. Planned to. Didn't happen."

April said nothing.

"I kept coming back here, to climb all those mountains."

They had said hello to Pat briefly, on the second day. Kevin had told her later that Pat was a mountaineer, and came from Ireland. He had had a chat with her while April was sleeping off the jet lag. He had befriended another group as well, four Austrians, undergrads like them – three guys and a girl, a brother and sister, and two cousins. The girl, Julia, was quite pretty. It was with this group that Kevin had gone white water rafting.

"Did you go climbing with friends?" April asked Pat.

"Not really," said Pat. "I made friends when I started climbing. I made great friends. My first husband, he wasn't into it. He came a couple of times and then he stayed home. Now Fred, my second, he's different. Loves climbing. I met him in Germany, when I was doing the Harz Mountains."

"But he didn't come this time," said April.

"Nope," said Pat. "Had hip replacement surgery four months ago. I'm afraid his climbing days may be over. And perhaps mine as well." She looked at her ankle.

"A serious fracture?" April asked.

"We'll know when the plaster comes off," Pat said. "It's not complicated, they say, but you never know."

April wondered how she could sound so upbeat about it all.

"But you, my dear, you should be getting about," said Pat. "In fact, I've arranged a little change of scene for you."

April looked at her, askance.

"I think you'll like it," said Pat confidently. "You know Neeta?"

April shook her head.

"She's the woman who sits at the tourist desk."

April remembered the smiley Nepali woman in local costume, whom she had seen at a desk labelled Tourist Information, in one corner of the lobby, a couple of times. On the second day, she seemed to have brought her daughter with her, a pretty, little girl who looked about five. She stared at April, then hid herself behind her mother's chair, and peeped out.

"She has a little girl," said April.

"Jaya is her granddaughter," said Pat. "I'll write their names down for you. Neeta's going to the Vajrayogini temple at Samkhu tomorrow morning. It's an interesting place, and not very far. It's on a small hill. Neeta will go by car to the base. She'll take you if you'd like to go."

April wondered what she should say.

"Will the little girl be there?" she asked.

"Possibly, she's often with Neeta," Pat replied. "There's a reason why Neeta goes up there. She'll probably tell you about it. The Vajrayogini is an important Buddhist deity, and the setting is lovely. You'll see."

"All right," said April. "I guess I'll go."

They set off at 9 a.m. the next morning, in a serviceable fiat. Neeta, Jaya and April sat in the back, the driver in front. The car drove slowly though Thamel, past old, wooden houses, hotels and temples, congested squares where people sold fresh vegetables and flowers, clothes and artifacts, cell phones and CDs, right in the street. There were other shopkeepers too, sitting in their little shops, their wooden or tin doors hanging open, selling household and electronic goods, silk paintings, shoes, toys.

While walking through this area on the second day, April had noticed the difference between the two trades. While the roadside sellers stood or squatted, talking loudly and gesturing, the shopkeepers displayed a solemn dignity. Their customers squeezed into the little shops, pointing out goods that interested them. Then the shopkeepers would take them off the shelf and display the wares on the counter.

Out on the street it was a jumble, a mass of indistinguishable objects, people, animals, a stray dog, or goat or cow, and motorcycles, scooters, cars, vans, bicycles, hand-drawn carts, all sharing the same space.

On the second day they had drifted into a couple of temples, looked into shops, before having lunch on the terrace of a Chinese restaurant. The thick, dark brown, high-smelling hot and sour soup she had ordered had made her sick, April was positive. Though the noodle dish Kevin had eaten did not bring trouble.

Slowly the car drove through the congested streets till the landscape became not unlike the suburban sprawl they had come through from the airport. They went along a road with larger, more spaced out houses, some with walls around them. Uniformed men, presumably guards, sat outside the closed, metal gates. Every now and then, April saw an apartment block. She noticed quite a few half constructed houses, with stacks of bricks lined up nearby. She saw too that it was cleaner here than in Thamel.

They got on a less populated road and soon the white, squat dome of the Boudhanath Stupa, with its flame-like, yellow spire loomed into view. April saw Neeta's hands come together. She closed her eyes and bowed her head. The Stupa was one of the essential sights, according to the guidebook.

They had not spoken since they had left the hotel, April marvelling at the ability for stillness and silence that not only Neeta, but little Jaya possessed as well.

She was thankful for it. She was getting better, but was not fully well yet.

Green rice fields with women bent low over them, here and there, little mud huts some distance away from the road, herds of goats, large spreading trees, and a much more bumpy road signalled an end to the city.

Neeta turned to her and said. "Do you know who the Vajrayogini is?"

April shook her head. She had meant to read the relevant section in *Lonely Planet* the night before, but had not got around to it. She felt somewhat embarrassed.

"She is a very important goddess for us Buddhists," said Neeta. "She represents clarity of thought and action. She is a depiction of our own enlightened nature, our true nature."

April was taken aback by the sudden revelation of these momentous seeming ideas, which had come without a prelude. She tried to take them in, nodding and smiling.

Soon they were in the little village of Samkhu, announced by a signpost. April saw many old wood and brick buildings in what she knew was the Newari style of architecture. In Kathmandu the structures had been more elaborate, decorated with intricate carvings and topped by a series of slanted roofs, stacked one on top of the other, sometimes ending in a small, golden dome. Here they were smaller, but the carved woodwork looked equally old and beautiful.

Then they were climbing a flight of rough-hewn, stone steps, passing small shrines, which were no more than painted, shapely stones with offerings of flowers and rice. Here and there was a small pond. Some of the route was well shaded. April loved the sudden appearance of greenery, and not just along the path and overhead. When they went by the exposed mountainside, a vista of green, paddy fields spread below them, with the dusty, little road they had taken curving through it.

Neeta asked her if she wanted to stop for a rest. April declined. Neeta and Jaya did not look tired either. A sturdy little girl, April thought approvingly. She took a few swigs from her water bottle, than they continued climbing.

Soon they were at a shrine. It consisted of a massive triangular stone with a hooded snake curving above it. It was smeared with red paste, and there were the usual offerings.

Neeta stood, her head bowed, praying. Jaya stood by her side, watching.

April felt disappointed. This was it? She had expected a proper temple.

And there was, a little higher up. The graceful Newari buildings of the type she had seen in Kathmandu reappeared, this time with tiered, copper-covered roofs. Neeta and Jaya took off their sandals at the entrance and April followed.

The Vajrayogini temple was the centre-most building. The figure she saw inside had a serene face, but her stance was warlike. She had many arms, one holding a gilt sword, while others held a chopper and a bowl shaped like a skull. She was dressed in a flowing, silky skirt. Among her jewellery was a garland of skulls and under her feet lay two prostrate figures. Seven statues of Buddha-like figures, tranquil and meditative, surrounded her. April stared, fascinated.

What could it all mean, she mused. She had not expected skulls and swords.

"Cutting through illusion." The sentence suddenly formed in her mind. "Cleaving through ignorance." She recalled reading something like that once, in a

Buddhist magazine at a friend's house. The sword would make sense then, metaphorical sense. What had Neeta said? "She represents clarity of thought and action." Could the skulls be death of ignorance, or ignorance itself?

April focussed on the Vajrayogini's face. Her eyes seemed intelligent, alive, and there was a gentleness there, and serenity. Yes, there was definitely a kind light in them. April felt that the Vajrayogini was looking directly at her, transmitting a kind of radiance through her glance. The experience was intensely corporeal. She was held in thrall by that immutable figure, aware at the same time that the space she was in was somehow timeless.

Then she was back in the temple. Well, she hadn't been anywhere, but somehow she had been in a dimension of another sort. It was hard to put it in words. Now she came to the realization that she was looking at a statue, an object not a living form. And she became aware of a strong scent of incense. But the moment of intimacy continued to hold her in its power.

She had an image flash though her mind – she was in grandmother's house, curled up on the comfy, old sofa, wrapped in a blanket, reading a comic book, and sipping warm apple cider.

April closed her eyes and said a little prayer, something she had not done since her childhood. Her mother had disappeared early from her life, and her prayers had dried up soon after.

Later in the car, on their way back, Neeta told her a story. "You know," she began, opening a packet of cookies and offering them around, "it was my mother who brought me to the Vajrayogini. She went through hard times, my mother, very hard times."

"What happened?" April asked.

"My father's family owned land, but his brother, my uncle, gambled and lost all the land, and even sold off the other investments. Luckily my father was BA. My father and mother came to Kathmandu and he got a job in a bank, but only after my mother had gone and prayed to the goddess. She was from a village near Samkhu. She had gone so many times to the temple, so many, but had never asked for anything. But that one time she did. She prayed hard. The women from her village told her that she must go there and pray. And after she did that, my parent's luck changed."

"Wow," April said.

Neeta nodded. She nibbled at her biscuit, and continued: "And me, I am fine. My husband has the hotel. He has other businesses. No money problems. But I was not having any children. Nothing for three years, till my mother brought me to the Vajrayogini. She is very powerful. But you must believe also, and try to follow her path."

"I loved it up there," April said. "Thank you for taking me."

"Oh, it is nothing," Neeta said. "I go at least once a month."

She said no more after that and April did not ask her any questions. Her thoughts had turned to Kevin.

He has gone right away to a little medical store near their hotel and got her the pills for her stomach flu, instructing her on what to do and what to avoid, adding to the advice she had got from the Travel Clinic in Toronto. Even so, he shouldn't have abandoned her. So what if Pat was around. After all, she didn't know Pat. Kevin was like that; he always put himself first. And he had a thing for white-water rafting; it was his favourite sport. But they were not in Canada, and he should have known better.

That evening, she went to a nearby restaurant for dinner, and met a group of young Australians who were headed north, to Mustang, on the Nepal–China border, an area dominated by Tibetan culture. This was their second trip to Nepal.

"The people are nice here," said Susan, a slim, tall blonde.

April agreed. She sat sipping tepid beer, content, listening to tales of adventure sports – mountain biking, trekking, paragliding, deep sea diving – in Australia and Asia, tales told not boastfully, but energetically, laughingly.

When she got back to the hotel, the man at the check-in desk told her that Pat was in the courtyard, waiting for her. The courtyard was pleasantly lit with low slung, Chinese lanterns that cast a warm, yellow glow all around. Pat sat in the same seat as before, wrapped in a dark shawl, smoking a water pipe.

"I am the Queen of this realm," she said gaily. Waving April into a chair, she offered her the pipe.

"It's just tobacco," she said. "Apple flavoured."

April took a puff. The scented smoke that entered her lungs was refreshing. Exhaling, she smiled at Pat. "Thanks."

"So what did you think of the Vajrayogini?" Pat asked.

April, expecting the question, had rehearsed for it. "It was really interesting," she had planned to respond. Instead she said: "I felt something."

"Did you?" Pat looked keenly at her.

April nodded solemnly.

"I'm glad," said Pat, smiling broadly. "I had hoped something like that would happen, but ..." She shrugged.

"I feel good," said April simply.

Pat sat back in her chair and took a deep puff.

"When I first came here, it was 1960, and I was 20."

April felt as if they were both in a tent, lit by a single oil lamp, somewhere on a high plateau, with a mighty wind blowing.

"There were some hippies here already then, plus researchers, explorers, all sorts of people. I had finished high school, worked, saved, and had come down with a few friends. Didn't know what I was going to do next."

April nodded.

"I felt really out of sorts when I got here. Had just broken up with a boyfriend. Didn't want to do drugs and all that. Not really. Didn't want to see the sites. So there I was, sitting pretty much where you are sitting now, moping, when Pushpa came to me. I knew her as this large lady in a saree that I had seen at the reception, Neeta's mother in fact. She told me, in broken English, that I should go somewhere with her. I had no idea what she was saying and I was not interested. She called Neeta, who must have been, what, 10 or something. She had much better English. That's how I ended up going to the Vajrayogini temple, with Pushpa and Neeta."

Pat paused for another long puff.

"I went out of boredom really and because they were being kind. And then, I had an experience. I did indeed. Didn't tell anyone about it back home. Though I talked about it to people here. After that visit, I signed up to go on a trek to the Annapurna base camp. Again, for no good reason. We had to go to Pokhran first; that's where they start. Twenty days it took then, walking in the shadow of that mighty mountain, sleeping in little hamlets each night. Twenty days of bliss. Ah."

Pat looked at April, her eyes shining.

"It wasn't easy. My shoes weren't quite right. I had calluses on my feet, and I ached here and I ached there. Though I was in good shape. Had a lot to learn, a hell of a lot. My mind though, my mind was wide open, and calm and light, just as it had been, for a few moments, in the Vajrayogini temple."

Pat gazed down at her left hand, which lay limp on her lap.

"I knew then that I wanted to be with the mountains, the mountains and the sky, as much as possible. When I went back home I took up nursing. It just came to me. Worked in a hospital, and gave private care. With that and a little bit my granduncle left me, it's been all right."

She paused again and looked straight at April, right into her eyes.

"Before you go away," she said, "go to Pokhran. Or somewhere else. But go on a trek. Go for more than a week, if you can. The mountains, you have to see the mountains up close."

"Go with Kevin?" April asked.

"Tell him that's what you want to do, if that's what you want to do."

April drew a deep breath. She did not know how things were going to be with Kevin. Would she forgive him? She did not know. They had three months ahead of them. She felt differently now, and that was unlikely to change.

"It was wonderful just being on that hill," she said. For a moment, the green landscape as they were climbing the hill shimmered before her eyes.

"She's smart, the Vajrayogini. Got herself a nice spot."

"She's kind too," said April shyly. What was she saying?

"Yes that too."

April sat up straight. "Do you think," she said. "Do you think that there's really something there?"

"There's her," said Pat.

"No, I mean …"

"Are you asking me if I believe in God? In other worldly things?" asked Pat. "I don't know. I really don't. But I can't deny what I felt in that temple, not just once, but almost every time I've been there. And I know what I feel when I am in the mountains. But I don't have a shrine at home. I have prayed to her, though, when I have been in tough spots."

"And?" said April.

"And nothing," said Pat. "There haven't been any miracles. I just felt good. Like you said yourself. More confident. And I've survived. More than survived. I've thrived. That's good enough for me. It's more than enough."

April smiled.

"I think I'll go to bed," she said.

"Sleep well," said Pat.

"I really want to thank you, but I don't know how."

Pat bowed her head. "Take my address, and send me a postcard. After you've seen more of Nepal."

April paused at the door and looked back. Pat's head rested against the back of the chair. With her eyes closed, she seemed to be drawing in the very essence of the starry night.

Another kind of goddess, April reflected, as she went in and up the stairs, light in foot and spirit.

The Room

Vicky has style, Suj thought, as she watched him roll a joint. Among their friends, he was the only one with a tobacco pouch and cigarette paper. He even had a lighter. The others pulled the tobacco out of a cigarette, added hash, and then coaxed the mixture back into the cigarette, making a bit of a mess in the process. Vicky's approach was more professional.

Vicky impaled the tiny ball of hash on a matchstick and set it alight. It released a familiar, mossy-sweet smell.

"I better open the window," said Suj.

"This is really good stuff," said Vicky, smiling the unfettered smile of the satisfied customer.

Light streamed into the room as Suj pushed back the faded green curtain and threw open the rickety windows. One of the hinges was loose; and the right windowpane hung a little lopsided. Maybe she should mention it to Madan.

Suj cancelled out the thought even as it formed. She wanted as little interaction with Madan as possible. And in any case, it was none of her business how Madan's uncle chose to maintain his flat.

She glanced at the narrow courtyard, three storeys below. It looked slimy, partially covered with water from a leaking tap. And it was littered with rotting vegetable peels, paper, crushed cardboard boxes, plastic bags and junk. She turned away in disgust.

Vicky had finished making the joint. As he inhaled, he narrowed his eyes, tossing back a lock of hair and furrowing his brow in a filmi way.

Suj studied her lover – unruly hair grown out almost to the shoulders, a slight beard, the whisper of a moustache, and an aquiline nose. He looked good, she decided. A bit like Vinod Khanna. Vinod was not her favourite Bollywood film star, but he was quite cute, with sexy eyes and a cleft on his chin.

Vicky passed the joint. Suj inhaled, willing herself not to cough. The problem was that she had never smoked cigarettes, graduating straight to hash. Exhaling, she swallowed rapidly, trying to soothe her itchy throat.

Vicky was reclined on the dusty rug, pillowing his head with his arms, his eyes dreamy. It's amazing how fast he gets hit, thought Suj. She drew on the joint again, more prepared for its harshness this time, and looked around the room.

There was a large, cheap-looking, brown sofa; two slightly-scratched, straight-backed wooden chairs and a low, round table with a patterned tablecloth. On it sat a vase with plastic flowers. A side table was piled with magazines. On the peeling, grey-blue walls were framed pictures of Hindu gods, and a family portrait. The overall effect was hideous.

She lay down, head resting on Vicky's chest, the white ceiling a relief to her eyes. She felt a bit hungry. Hash always did that to her. She had a half-eaten cheese sandwich in her lunchbox, but she didn't want to finish that. She longed for something tongue-tickling, like *pav-bhaji*.

Vicky started stroking her hair. Suj wanted to close her eyes and give herself up to the sensation, but she couldn't take her eyes off the red, plastic roses with their dark green leaves, sitting smugly in the tarnished brass vase.

"Wouldn't it be great if we could redesign this room?" she said, turning over and stroking Vicky's arm. "Paint these walls … off-white maybe. Get nice furniture. Put in new curtains, posters on the walls. It's such an awful place."

"It's not so bad," said Vicky, stroking her neck. "Has its uses, doesn't it?"

"Guess so," said Suj, cuddling up.

Suddenly the hash hit her and she was off, a balloon with a happy face, adrift in the sky. She had a vision of Juhu beach at dusk, a mud-red sun low on the horizon, nearly gone, everything changing form — the food carts, the street children jumping around in the waves, the stray dog skulking by. The solid lines started becoming indistinct, as the light dimmed, and the indeterminate hues between day and night came into play.

Vicky's caresses were getting more urgent. She had a last coherent thought before she plunged into a sea of sensuality. Light yellow would be better for the walls than off-white, setting off the chequered, old, black and white floor, the only decent thing about the room.

A light breeze was coming in through the window when Suj resurfaced. It was so much nicer than the fan, which circulated stale, warm air. She consulted her watch. Quarter to four. She brushed her lips against Vicky's cheek and whispered: "Vicky, Vicks." Vicky did not stir.

Suj sat up, shaking her hair out of her eyes, stretching. She smoothened her *kameez*. It looked a bit crushed. It would be easy to conceal the creases under her *dupatta*, which was carefully draped over one of the chairs.

She touched Vicky's shoulder and said: "Vikram."

Vicky opened his eyes slowly. Smiling, he slipped his hand into hers.

"We should start getting ready," Suj said.

"Ohhhhh," Vicky yawned. "Madan's uncle never gets here before five, if he comes at all."

"But we had decided that we'd leave an hour's margin."

"I know, but it isn't even four yet. We can stay till then."

Suj turned away, frowning.

"Relax, sweetie. Show me your sketch book," Vicky said.

He leafed through sketches and watercolours of gardens, flowers, trees, and the sea.

"I like this one," he said.

He had paused at a watercolour of a fabulous, old *Peepal* (fig) tree, incredibly gnarled and twisted, with a little red, rounded stone at its base that represented Lord Ganesh. Suj had captured well the effect created by the late afternoon light coming through its ample canopy of heart-shaped, dark green leaves.

A smile brightened Suj's dark, pixie face. She liked to draw and paint natural things; she aspired to paint landscapes. It was scenes of gushing waterfalls, orange sunsets and misty mountains that had drawn her to art. But landscapes were not trendy, she had found out at the art class she was taking. Her teacher was not interested in them, nor were any of her classmates. Nevertheless, Suj nursed her passion the best she could, hunting down books on landscape and nature painting in the library of the St. Xavier's College, where she and Vicky were doing their Bachelors. She couldn't afford art books, and treasured the slim book on Turner's seascapes that Vicky had given her on her 18th birthday. He had bought it for eight rupees from the hawkers near Flora Fountain, after some bargaining.

At college the next day, Suj had finished her class and was going to meet Vicky in the canteen, when she ran into Madan.

"Coming to the canteen?" he asked.

"I'm going to the library," she improvised.

"You work too hard, *yaar*," Madan said mockingly. "You should have more fun."

Suj turned away and walked stiffly to the library, sitting down with a heavy volume entitled *3000 Years of Indian Art and Sculpture*. She was fuming. What a creep!

She had disliked Madan on sight, since the first day she had met him in history class. Sitting in one of the front rows, he had surveyed her from top to toe when she had walked in. He had a broad face, with a sallow complexion, and oily hair. He reminded her of a pig. There was often a hint of scorn or malice in his eyes.

Suj found herself staring at a full-page illustration of Natraj. "Bronze, 5th century, the Chola period," read the caption. Madan must be in the canteen now, chatting with Vicky, telling him that he had run into Suj. Maybe he was saying something lewd about the fact that Vicky and Suj had gone to the flat the day before? And how was Vicky responding? With laughter? Anger shot through Suj – a flaming arrow.

How weird it was that Vicky and Madan got along well. They had lived in the same neighbourhood and played cricket together in their back lane, as children. Perhaps Madan had not been so bad as a child, thought Suj. But he had definitely turned out horrible.

As she was leaving the library, she ran into Tina.

"Are you coming to Matheran?" Tina asked her.

Oh shoot, thought Suj, she had clean forgotten her friend Malini's birthday celebration, which was to take place that weekend, at her cottage in the nearby hill resort.

"I have not asked my folks yet," she answered. "But I will tonight."

There was no one in the one-bedroom flat that Suj shared with her parents and sister when she let herself in, a couple of hours later. Her mother must have gone out somewhere. It was nice to have the place to herself, for a change. Suj turned on the radio and started making tea. The radio sang: *Toote hua khwabo nein, humko yeh sikhaya hain ... This is what broken dreams have taught me ...*

What would she put in her still life? The assignment was due in a couple of days. She didn't want to paint fruit in a bowl, or a vase of flowers. Nor those typical, heavy drapes as a backdrop. What then? Opening the fridge to get milk, Suj encountered some vegetables. There was eggplant, *karela* (bitter gourd), carrots, spinach and tomatoes. Suj was struck by them. She pulled them out and started arranging them on the dining table. She needed more light. Going to the window, she pulled the curtains way back. What colours, she thought, putting the eggplant against the spinach. And what textures – she caressed the tomatoes, plump and smooth. Could the veggies be the subject of her still life?

Suj made herself a cup of tea and sat gazing at them, wondering what she would use as a backdrop, when Sheetal, her elder sister, came in.

"Hi Sujata," she said. "Is there tea?"

Suj looked absently at her. "I only made one cup."

"Oh. I better make some more then," said Sheetal. "Did you boil the potatoes?"

"What?"

"I'd told you this morning to boil potatoes when you came back from college." Sheetal's voice rose impatiently when she saw Suj's blank stare.

"But I just came back myself, ten minutes ago."

"You could have put the potatoes on after you came back."

"I'll do them now."

"And what are all these vegetables doing on the table?"

"I … they … I'll put them back."

Sheetal gave Suj an irritated look as she left the room.

Suj set about boiling more water for the potatoes. She considered them carefully. Should there be a potato or two in the still life? Or would that make the composition too cluttered? Suj left the vegetables on the table. She would put them away soon. It was no use telling Sheetal about the still-life assignment; she had no interest in art. She had a Bachelors in Commerce and worked in a bank. Sheetal did not approve of Suj's plan to go to the J.J. School of Fine Arts, after she finished her B.A. Suj was spaced out as it was. Suj's compromise was doing a B.A. before she went to art school. Her parents had insisted that a practical degree precede the other one.

That evening, Suj approached her mother during a commercial break, when she was watching her favourite serial, and told her about Malini's birthday celebration.

"Go *beta*," her mother said. "And don't forget your sweater."

Suj's heart leapt with joy. It was going to be such fun! There was so much to sketch in Matheran, most of all, monkeys!

When the phone rang, Suj ran to answer. It was Vicky. How many times had she told him not to call at home? He was too impulsive; he just didn't get it.

"We're planning to go to the disco Saturday night," he said. "Want to come?"

"I am going to Matheran," Suj said. "It's Malini's birthday and all the girls are going."

"Really? You didn't tell me."

"I just decided today."

"Oh shit. We could have gone dancing. You've been wanting to."

"I can sketch in Matheran. I can never sketch the things I want to, in Bombay."

"We could go to the disco on Saturday and go to Matheran next weekend."

"I don't know. I wish you'd asked earlier. Malini will really mind if I don't go."

Vicky was silent. He was easily hurt.

"Look. I'll make a special picture just for you. And we'll go to the disco soon, I promise." She did not want to go to Matheran with Vicky, alone. It would be too intimate.

"Okay," Vicky said, sounding put out.

As they hung up, she decided that she would be extra sweet to him the next day.

Matheran was beautiful. Malini's parents' bungalow was old, graceful and incredibly spacious. Suj counted 4 bedrooms, and there was a wide veranda that ran all around the house. Plus there were the servants quarters at the back, and a large garden. To think that such a big house was empty most of the time!

First there had been the early morning train journey from Bombay to Neral, then the 5-hour hike to Matheran. They were in high spirits, joking and singing on their way up. It had rained the night before, and Matheran was wonderfully cool, green and misty. They arrived around 1:30, absolutely famished, despite the snacks consumed en route. Shobhatai, the maid who doubled as a cook, had a delicious meal all ready for them.

After the meal they went out on the veranda and Meeta glimpsed a green and black striped snake in the foliage, generating much excitement. Then the monkeys paid a visit. They sat on the compound wall, scratching their heads, their brown eyes alert in their small, almost-human faces. Three of them scampered onto the veranda, causing the girls to scream and scatter. Then they all took off, swinging casually from branch to branch, their long tails dangling down.

After their departure, the girls sprawled on the easy chairs in the veranda. There were eight of them – Suj, Tina, Malini, Shirin, Meeta, Shaheen, Papadi and Laxmi.

"Malini should make a birthday speech," Tina suggested.

"Who me? I have nothing to say," Malini protested.

"Eat, drink and be merry, for tomorrow ye die," said the irrepressible Shirin.

"You forgot sex." Papadi introduced her favourite topic.

"You're so one-track," Shirin said. "Besides, it's included in the merry part."

"You left out love, anyhow," Shaheen said. She was a romantic who usually had her nose stuck inside a Mills and Boons.

"What about virginity?" Shirin asked idly, slumping further in her chair.

"Virginity is a load of crap," Papadi said.

"It isn't!" Shaheen said. "It's important to be a virgin till you're married. That's what makes your *suhaag raat* special."

"Not really," Papadi said. "It's painful the first time. Very."

Everyone was listening intently now.

"How do you know that?" challenged Shaheen.

"Come on, everybody knows that," Papadi said.

"Everyone but Shaheen," Malini said, sitting up in her chair.

"It's because of the hymen," Laxmi said in a conspiratorial tone. "My sister said it was hell the first time. She and her husband never went all the way on their first night. It was almost a week before they actually did it."

Confession followed confession.

"You know what my cousin did?" Tina said. "She and her fiancé started making out a couple of months before they got married. That way they had a good *suhaag raat*."

"Hear and learn, Shaheen," Shirin said.

"I'm not going to have sex before I am married, no matter what," Shaheen responded.

"Why all this fuss about the silly hymen? Screw it!" Papadi said, feeling that she had kept quiet too long.

"I'm sure you're going to, Papadi," Shaheen said scornfully.

"How's your husband going to know?" Shirin said. "Women break their hymen doing sporty things, like horse riding. There's no way to tell for sure."

"Still, your husband may get suspicious if you don't bleed, no?" Laxmi suggested.

"That's his problem," Papadi said.

"I have been horse riding right here in Matheran," Malini said.

"Most of us probably have a ruptured hymen any-way," Papadi pronounced.

"I don't think so," Shaheen said. "I don't play any sports."

"Oh Shaheeeen, you're so purrre, like the snow on Mount Evereeeest!" Shirin sang.

"You know your husband will mind if you're not a virgin, even if he doesn't say anything," Shaheen replied, stung.

"Maybe your husband will like it if you're a bit experienced," Papadi suggested.

"I'm sure your marriage will be very happy then," Shaheen said.

"Bitch," Papadi said, flinging a cushion at her.

"Stop it you two," Malini said. "Let's play cricket. Where are the stumps?"

They played cricket in a desultory fashion, till 4 o'clock, when Shobhatai served tea and snacks. Then they went for a long walk. Suj kept falling behind as she paused to sketch, every so often. Finally she split up from the group and sat down to sketch at Sunset Point.

By the time she returned, a drinking session had commenced. Tina had stolen two half-full bottles – whisky and rum – from her father's bar. Since she had two elder brothers, any untoward occurrences in her house were always attributed to them. Shaheen, an observant Muslim, was sipping a Fanta.

They didn't stay up very late after dinner. They went to bed after they had given Malini her presents, and she had opened and admired them. They couldn't even summon the energy to give her birthday bumps. All the physical activity, healthy air, lavish food and drink, had brought on early fatigue.

Suj woke up a few hours later, feeling thirsty. She went to the kitchen and had a drink. Moonlight bathed the garden and a section of the veranda. She let herself out as quietly as she could and sat down on the steps. The silence was incredible, accentuated by the chirp of a cricket, every so often. It was almost full moon. A line of trees, tall and jagged, cut strong patterns against the deep blue sky. The clouds had cleared up completely. The starlit sky was incredibly beautiful. Suj had not seen a sight like this for ages. Bombay was such an awful place; chock-a-block with people and buildings and more people and buildings. The only nice thing about it was the sea.

She heard soft footsteps and saw Malini come out on the veranda. She came and sat down beside her. They were silent for a few minutes, then started a whispered conversation.

"That was a funny, this afternoon," Malini said.

"Yeah," Suj responded.

"You didn't say anything."

"Didn't know what to."

"Do you think anyone has ... done it?"

"Wouldn't they tell us?"

"You never know with these things. It's all so confusing."

"It's terrible. I don't want to go all the way. But ..."

"Has Vicky said anything?"

"No. Has Neelesh?" Suj was referring to Malini's boyfriend.

"No. He is too scared, I think. So am I."

"Vicky wants us to come to Matheran."

"Alone?"

"Yeah."

"And you?"

"I don't know. I said no."

"It's better that way."

There was silence again.

"Do you feel pressured sometimes?" Malini asked.

Suj considered the question. "I think I do," she said. "From my own body."

Malini looked at her admiringly. "You're so honest."

Suj said nothing. She thought of the room. No, she wasn't that honest.

"That's what comes through in some of your drawings," Malini added.

"Really?" Suj felt very flattered; this was the greatest compliment she had ever got.

"Yeah," Malini said.

A few more moments passed.

"I don't think I'm ready," Malini said.

"Nor me."

"We'll know when we are."

"I think so."

Back in Bombay, a couple of days passed before Vicky suggested the room again. It was always Vicky who got the keys from Madan. But Vicky called Suj at home that morning.

"Listen," he said. "I can't make it to college. My dad wants me to do some stuff. But we can still go. Get the keys from Madan and meet me at Charni Road station at 2 o'clock. Okay?"

Suj was furious. She wanted to refuse, but Vicky would ask for an explanation and she couldn't talk when her parents were within earshot. How dare he call her at home and say all this?

"Yeah," she managed to say. She went back to the table, but couldn't finish her breakfast. She was so mad she felt she'd choke on the food. She sat around sipping her tea, pretending to read the paper, till everyone got up. Then she dumped what was left of her breakfast in the dustbin. She wasn't going to talk to Madan. No way.

She ran to get her bag from her room. The sketch she had made in Matheran for Vicky lay on her desk. She had planned to give it to him today. Suj was seized by the urge to take hold of it and rip it up. But she just kept going.

Madan sat two rows behind her in class. During the lecture, she felt his eyes boring into her back. He knew they were supposed to go to the flat that day and was waiting for her to ask him for the keys, the creep. She hated his fat, stupid face. She wanted to land a fist right on his ugly nose. The fact that she had got her still-life assignment back the night before, and her marks were good, did not help. The day was in ruins, the wreckage littered around her feet.

She was hungry at the end of the lecture and decided to get something to eat. She bought a plate of *batata-wadas* in the canteen and sat down at an empty table. It was almost lunch time and the place was filling up. Suddenly, Madan appeared and sat down next to her, a bottle of Limca in his hand, a broad grin on his face. Suj shrank instinctively against the wall, experiencing the funny, hollowness in the chest that she sometimes felt on entering an examination hall.

"So," Madan said.

She ignored him and looked around the room. She could feel his hateful gaze boring into her again. He was making her feel like, like what, a whore?

One of her *wadas* lay uneaten on her plate, but she had no appetite for it anymore.

She looked up and met his gaze. She was going to tell him off, once and for all. She had had enough of this kind of behaviour.

A cruel, little smile played on Madan's lips. Suj's heart was beating very fast. Suddenly she felt a rush of panic. She was trapped between Madan and the wall. Trapped and suffocating. For an appalling moment, her eyes remained locked into his. Then she willed herself to look away and get up.

"Excuse me," Suj said, her voice emerging unnaturally from her dry throat.

Madan got up and made room for her to pass, his face a sneering mask. She brushed against him as she moved, even though she tilted her body the other way, as far as it would go. Shuddering, she rushed out of the canteen, through the hallway, down a short flight of steps, out of the building. She looked back, sweating and out of breath, half expecting to see Madan. But he was nowhere in sight. God, how scared she had been back there. How glad she was to get away.

Vicky greeted her cheerfully at the ticket window at Charni Road.

"*Chalo*, let's go," he said.

"Where?" asked Suj. She had tried to get hold of herself on the commuter train, but now she felt her composure unravelling.

"What do you mean?"

"I mean where do you want to go?" Suj demanded.

"Didn't you get the keys?"

"Of course not," Suj screamed. "You know how much I hate talking to Madan."

"I don't believe this. You mean you didn't get the keys?" Vicky's voice had risen too.

"No I did not." People were beginning to look at them.

"Let's go," said Vicky grimly. He clasped Suj so tightly by her arm that it hurt. He led her out of the station. Suj struggled to free her arm from Vicky's grasp. He let go, refusing to look at her. They started walking down the road, the sullen sun beating down on them.

"You know Suj, you're carrying this I-hate-Madan business too far," Vicky said angrily. "I don't know how you can be so stupid."

Suj didn't say anything. Her body felt bloated with poisonous substances; maybe she would burst.

"Let's sit down somewhere," said Vicky.

Suj followed Vicky into an Irani restaurant. They took a corner table. A minute passed before they looked at each other.

"What's the problem? Why can't you talk to Madan?" Vicky demanded.

Suj shook her head silently.

"First you're unreasonable. Then you won't even explain yourself," said Vicky, emphasizing each word as if he were addressing a child.

The waiter came over with two glasses of water, and took a cold drink order from Vicky.

How happy she had been in Matheran and the day after she had got back, thought Suj. And it had been a relief to talk to Malini.

An image of the bungalow formed in her mind, soon overlaid by the room, with its lumpy, old sofa, the gaudy, plastic flowers, and the broken window, always hatefully the same. She didn't want to think about it. She didn't ever want to go there again.

Before the room they had to go all the way to Bandstand for some privacy, necking with many other couples in view. Or they sat on the sea wall on Marine Drive, exchanging furtive caresses and hasty kisses, always afraid of being seen. Then Madan had got hold of a set of keys to his uncle's bachelor pad, saying that he needed a quiet place to study. He had told Vicky about it, and Vicky has asked Madan if they could use it sometimes.

The drink arrived. After taking a sip, Vicky pushed the bottle towards her. Suj drank some of the cool, coke-like liquid. Then she drank some more.

"Look," she said, steadily holding his gaze. "I don't like Madan. That's it. I will not deal with him."

"I still find it stupid. But if you want it that way." Vicky shrugged.

"Yes, that's how I want it, " said Suj firmly.

They finished the coke in silence.

"Let's take a bus to Hanging Gardens," Vicky suggested.

They sat at the top of a double-decker, right in the front seat. There was a nice breeze and they had a great view of the streets.

"My father may buy me a mo-bike," Vicky said. "That's what he was saying. Wouldn't that be terrific? We could really go places." Suj nodded. Then she told him about her marks. She could see that he was impressed. Vicky took her hand and stroked it. Suj smiled at him.

They reached the Hanging Gardens and walked around hand in hand. The atmosphere was festive as usual, with vendors selling toys, balloons, food. A monkey show was in progress. It reminded Suj that she hadn't had the chance to draw the monkeys in Matheran.

They decided to sit down in the garden for a while, but it was too hot. None of the benches were adequately shaded.

"Let's go to the other side. It's nicer," Vicky said.

The Hanging Gardens were located on a small hill. They descended to Peddar Road through a series of terraces covered in thick foliage. Suj and Vicky took the path going down. Vicky had his arm around Suj. He was all sweaty and sweet, Suj wanted to hug him.

She wished they were back in the room. Leaning into Vicky, she nibbled on his earlobe.

Vicky led her off the path. They found a spot behind some bushes and sat down. They kissed fiercely, their arms tightly entwined. A few minutes passed.

"What's going on here?" A tall, well-built man in a khaki uniform had appeared out of nowhere. He stood over them, glaring, addressing them in Hindi.

"We ... we're just resting. It's so hot," said Vicky. Suj felt her heart beat erratically.

"Resting, eh? Who is this with you?" said the man aggressively. "Your wife?"

"She's ... a friend," Vicky said.

"Do you have identification?"

"Who're you? We're not doing anything wrong," Vicky insisted. "We're just resting."

"I am an army officer, you understand? What do you mean you're just resting? I saw what you were doing. You should be ashamed." The stranger's hostility hit Suj like the heat of a punishing sun.

"Sorry," she said, her voice shrinking. "We were about to go home."

"Go home? Where do you live?"

"Look, we were just resting and now we're going to go home," said Vicky evenly.

"A police station is where we will go," said the man, his voice rising. "Let's go right now."

"A police station? We are not doing any harm. What are you talking about?" Vicky was beginning to shout.

"Then what. Such shameless behaviour in public."

The man stood on top of Vicky and Suj, glaring. He had a thick moustache, and large, bulging eyes, in a fleshy face.

"Look, we're sorry," said Vicky in a quieter tone. "We didn't mean to offend anyone." He got up and helped Suj to her feet.

"Where are you going?" the man asked roughly. "You better give me your names and addresses. What will your parents think of all this?"

Vicky took out his wallet and extracted the single twenty-rupee note he had. "Let it be, okay?" he said.

The man pocketed the note. "Such shameless behaviour," he said. "What will your parents think? You should take your studies seriously."

They left him staring and muttering and walked rapidly down the path to Peddar road.

Suj glanced at Vicky. He was looking elsewhere, perhaps avoiding her gaze. She wanted him to say something, anything, but he did not. There was only the meaningless flow of afternoon traffic and people, with buildings jutting into the sky, many of them shopfronts with large glass windows that bounced back light, their interiors shadowy and distorted.

"Let's get a cab," said Vicky, with a quick glance at her. Suj nodded. She had just enough money for a short ride. She wanted to get away. Put the Arabian Sea between herself and the Hanging Gardens. The Indian Ocean would be even better. And she wanted to get away from Vicky and be alone.

She had had it. No more of this shit. She was going to join a Convent! Yes, that's what she was going to do. Then Suj remembered that she was Hindu.

Munni

There are no photographs of Munni, only her image, branded on my memory.

A stud enlivened her nose. You could divine her mood by studying her flared nostrils, when you couldn't read the expression in her large, dark eyes. They beamed their attention acutely on one thing at a time, not given to easy distraction. Her habitual expression was thoughtful.

Her waist-length hair was well oiled and firmly braided; two braids, ends tied with red ribbon, then looped, so that the ribbons appeared as large bows beside her ears. We used to call these braids *jilbi-veni*. *Jilbi* was a sticky, coiled, bright-orange sweet, accompanied by a glass of pungent buttermilk, served as breakfast every morning at the local sweet shop, only to the strong-hearted.

Munni (little girl), was tall for her age, and wore long skirts with waist-length, half-sleeved blouses, both cut from the same bright, floral-patterned, cheap cotton. I remember the rough texture of her clothes, while my own dresses, short, soft and frilly, were called frocks.

Her feet were usually bare: dusty, black feet, a little cracked at the soles. She would have to go and wash her hands and feet as soon as she came to our place. (This decree, issued by my grandmother, applied to everyone, shod or unshod, who came into the house from outside.) Later, when she travelled with us, she wore rubber, "Hawaii" *chappals*, which had a single, strong grip for the big toe.

I have little recollection of what I looked like at 10. The mirror was alien to me then. But the image of 12-year-old Munni is branded on my memory. Munni was my playmate and my baby brother's nanny, in that order, at least for me. I didn't distinguish between her two roles; after all, I too had responsibilities towards my little brother.

I see now that a chasm lay between us. Munni and I dealt with that difference with the ease of children skipping rope, counting to a 100 without missing a beat. If we met now, would we hesitate, and stumbling in our hesitation, draw back fearfully from the edge of a seeming precipice?

Munni's favourite game was hopscotch, which was known to us as *Billus*. When we played the game, she would hitch up her skirt, tucking many folds into her waistband. We played very seriously, with utmost focus. There was no fooling around. We often appointed a third person as an umpire.

I was partial to *Phugdi*, which consisted of two people facing each other, keeping their feet together and holding their hands crossed, at arms distance, then swirling madly in unison, feet tapping hard on the concrete floor of our veranda.

"Stop, stop!" I would be the first to say, as we would slow down gradually from what felt like a terrific speed. We would stagger to the wall and lean against it, giggling, euphoric. The game was particularly attractive since my grandmother forbade it, afraid that we would lose our balance and crash to the floor.

I was doing "craft" at school, and there was homework to be done in this, as in all the other subjects. Munni loved craft. At one time she had gone to a municipal school and completed Class Three. Then she had stayed home to look after her younger siblings and had been hired by my parents to take care of my brother.

She read aloud sometimes from my old Hindi textbook. The words rolled out slowly, with an effort. But Munni enjoyed reading; she would be transported for hours afterwards.

At our craft sessions we painted eggshells, and put them on twigs we had collected, to assemble decorative trees; we made papier-mâché bowls and painted them; we cut coloured paper into patterns, and worked with crayons and watercolours to make paintings of clowns, mountains, birds, houses, planes, people, whatever took our fancy.

After one such session, Munni took my brother for his bath and I started washing the brushes, palette and my black and purple hands in the kitchen sink, when my mother said to me in English: "Don't sit so close to Munni. She may have lice."

English had been a code language between my parents before I went to school. They used to talk about things like their evening plans that didn't include me, and other adult stuff, in English. It was also a language in which they would negotiate about my grandmother who was crafty enough to pounce on them and demand that they use only Marathi, our mother tongue, in her presence. As I became proficient in English, it no longer served these purposes. But it could still be used to hide things from the servants. Munni and I spoke in Hindi. I had no understanding of Telugu, Munni's mother tongue. I conversed with my grandmother solely in Marathi. I spoke with my parents in English and Marathi and with my baby brother in gibberish.

"She may have lice." The words echoed in my head for a couple of days. Why should Munni have lice? She washed her hair as often as I did.

Munni lived in a single room with her parents and four brothers and sisters, in the servant's quarters down the road. The quarters consisted of about a dozen, narrow rooms set in a row, with a common latrine and bathroom. They were a five-minute walk from our house, and a two-minute run. I could see Munni's house from our garage, which was behind our garden.

I went to her house once, and sampled the chili-hot food that her mother, who worked as a house-maid, cooked for the family. Sitting cross-legged on the floor, I ate Andhra-style rice and curry for the first time. I felt my tongue, then throat, chest and stomach, and ultimately my whole being, catch fire. Flames escaped from my mouth, and possibly my ears. I turned into a dragon, albeit a pitiful one. Tears streamed down my cheeks and choking sounds escaped my mouth. I was plied immediately with glasses of water and given a lump of jaggery to suck.

Sitting back from my plate, I watched Munni's father enviously. He rolled the rice and curry into a ball, held it for a moment in his palm, then tossed it directly into his mouth, bringing a juggler's effort-lessness to this task. I decided to imitate him. All the rice balls missed my mouth save one. It made eating so much more fun.

I did not mention my little adventure to anyone at home, knowing perhaps instinctively that it might not be well received.

Munni did not usually sleep at our house. She went home every evening at six thirty and came back the next morning around eight thirty. But on one occasion, Munni and my best friend Sharmila both stayed over at our house. My mother's night shift at the hospital, where she worked as a doctor, coincided with my father being out-of-town for work. My grandmother had recently had a stroke that had changed her from an active, vivacious woman into a zombie of sorts, who sat in a chair on the veranda for hours, staring into space. She could no longer look after my brother. So it fell to the three of us to ensure that the baby got fed and came to no harm.

Sharmila was the same age as Munni. She was a warm, curious, energetic girl who liked to bully me sometimes. She was an only child as I had been, until the recent, exciting arrival of my baby brother.

Sharmila was dropped off at our place punctually at eight and my mother departed for her night shift, trying till the last minute to get another doctor to replace her. She looked rather anxious, though we assured her that we were more than equal to our task. She called from the hospital at nine p.m. to check if everything was all right.

Half an hour later, having fed and changed my brother, and put him to sleep, we all went to bed. Something woke me up sometime later. I lay in bed, disoriented, staring incomprehensibly at the roof of the large, white mosquito net, which enveloped us like a tent. The sound of someone sobbing softly cut through the dark. I sat up in bed and so did Sharmila, who was sleeping next to me.

We slipped out from under the flaps of the mosquito net, careful not to open them too wide. If a mosquito got in it was quite a task to kill it.

Switching on the table lamp, I glanced across at my brother sleeping peacefully in his baby cot, under a smaller mosquito net. Then I turned towards Munni, who was sleeping on a mat, curled into a ball, face to the wall, her shoulders twitching as she sobbed.

Sharmila had already crawled over to her and was shaking her, trying to turn her around: *"Kya hua?"* she asked. *What happened?* Munni continued sobbing, resisting the attempt to be turned around. I looked at Sharmila, feeling completely at a loss.

We sat kneeling by Munni for a minute or so. Then I put a hand on her shoulder and whispered in Hindi: "Why are you crying? What's the matter?"

Munni turned around to face us. "Will you teach me English?" she asked.

I looked at Sharmila, not knowing what to say.

"Will you?" Munni asked again.

"Of course," I said quickly. "Do you want to learn English?"

"Yes, I want to learn English," Munni said.

"We'll teach you," Sharmila said. "It's very easy."

"You won't forget?" Munni said.

"No I won't," I replied, staring into Munni's eyes, which were reddish and swollen. Seizing the writing pad and pencil that were kept near the phone, I scribbled her name – M–U–N–N–I – on a page and gave it to her. Munni's face relaxed into a slight smile.

"Let's go back to sleep now or we might wake the baby," Sharmila whispered.

I slept badly after that, dreaming that various characters from my storybooks had all come together in a huge room. They were throwing food around, getting into scuffles, and chasing each other. The scene seemed to be inspired by a Laurel and Hardy movie that I had seen at the Club.

My family left that town in central India, soon after, to go and live in Calcutta – a strange and wondrous place. We didn't understand the language at first, or the customs. But we found them endlessly amusing and fascinating. Smells of fried fish rose up to our fourth floor apartment at all hours. My grandmother had died before our move to Calcutta. A strict vegetarian who would not touch eggs, she would not have appreciated these odours.

Munni came with us to Calcutta for a while. We would go for walks along the Dhakuria lakes near our house, excited by this proximity to water. The town where we had lived before was located in a dust bowl. West Bengal by contrast was wet and humid, a luscious green. Along the lakeshore were vendors selling mouth-watering new food – *zaal-mudi, puchka* and *aloo dum*.

Munni was sent back home after a month. She was at an awkward age, my mother said. Besides, it wasn't right to take her away from her family for long. We had only brought her along to help us settle down. My mother also mentioned that Munni would soon be married.

I never got around to teaching Munni English. I never saw her again.

I picked up lice in Calcutta from someone in my expensive, private school. I was finally allowed to cut my hair short and considered myself very cool. Photographs of myself with *jilbi-venis* disappear from the family photo albums around this time.

There are no photographs of Munni, only her image, branded on my memory.

Author Notes

The Bombay stories take place in the mid–1980s when Bombay had not yet been renamed Mumbai.

Zindagi Itefaq Hai refers to an old, Hindi, film song from the 1969 film *Aadmi aur Insaan*. Check out the duet on Youtube!

Glossary

All words are in Hindi, unless otherwise specified

Aai – mother (Marathi)

Aaji – grandmother (Marathi)

Attar – perfume

Behenji – Sister, a polite form of address

Beta – son/child

Bhagwat Geeta – a key Hindu philosophical and religious text

Bidis – crude cigarettes

Bindi – a dot on the forehead worn traditionally by Hindu women

Chaddi – underwear

Coolie – manual labourer, in this case a porter

Dupatta – a long scarf, sometimes draped around the head by women a mark of modesty

Ghats – a series of steps leading to a water body, usually a holy river.

Ghats (Western) – a mountain range that runs North-South along India's Western edge some distance inland

Gulli – an alley

Jigari dost – best buddy

Kaka – Uncle (Marathi)

Khadi – home-spun, rough cotton fabric popularized by Mahatma Gandhi during the Independence Movement as a symbol of India's self reliance.

Kheema – minced meat

Koto – a traditional, Japanese, stringed musical instrument. (Japanese)

Kurta – a long tunic, worn by men and women

Lafda – affair

Maidan – a large, open space often used for sports

Matherchoth – motherfucker

Mavshi – Maternal aunt (Marathi)

Miya – husband (Urdu)

Munni – little girl

Mushairya – event where a particular kind of Urdu poetry is recited

Namaste – traditional Hindu greeting done with with the palms touching and held upright at the level of the heart.

Paan – stuffed betel leaf concoction usually eaten after a meal.

Paanwalla – a maker and seller of paan.

Padmasan – sitting cross-legged in yoga in the lotus pose

Pallu – the end of the saree that hangs over the back.

Puja – a Hindu religious ritual

Pukka (road) – properly done, a tarred road

Salwaar-Kameez – traditional Indian costume for women, originating in North India

Satsang – religious gathering which can involve reading scriptures, singing, listening to a talk. It literally means in the company of truth.

Shayari – North Indian poetry and semi-classical music. The lyrics are often in Urdu.

Shlok – hymn (Sanskrit)

Suhaag raat – the first night that a married couple spends together has a cultural connotation in India and is often played up in Bollywood movies. A girl was expected to be a virgin on her suhaag raat.

Tatami – mat used as floor covering in a traditional Japanese house. (Japanese)

Tava – flat, iron griddle

Tikka – red vermillion powder mark made on the forehead and used to welcome guests. It also has a religious significance.

Yaar – friend

Acknowledgements

"Freire Stopped in Bombay" contains an excerpt from the poem "To be or not to be Born" by L.S. Rokade which appeared in *No Entry for the New Sun*, edited by Arjun Dangle, Disha Books, Orient Longman, India, 1992.

Lover Man (Oh, where can you be), 1942, Words and music: Jimmy Davis/Ram Ramirez/James Sherman.

Thank You:

Smita, for saying: "Enough! Get that book to a publisher." Marc-Antoine for turning Patron of the Arts and humble proofreader. Geneviève, Mom and Amar for unconditional support; Falguni for her enthusiasm and creative flair.

Michael Mirolla of Guernica Editions for always being receptive and ready to unveil the arcane practices of the publishing world!

And the Ontario Arts Council for a small grant under its Writers' Reserve Program in 1996.

Previously Published

"Munni," *Maple Tree Literary Supplement*. No. 8, 2011.

"Freire Stopped in Bombay," *Cerebration, a literary online journal of the Drew University*, Issue 4, 2005.

"Zindagi Itefaq Hai (Life is Chance)," *The Toronto Review of Contemporary Writing Abroad*, Winter 1998.

"Reveries of a Riot," *Diva, Quarterly Journal of South Asian Women*, 1993 and *Aurat Durbar, Writings by Women of South Asian Origin*, Second Story Press, Toronto, 1995.

Audio anthology: Snapshot, *EarLit Shorts 5*, audio-book anthology series, Rattling Books, Canada. Upcoming.

About The Book

"These are stories that provide the genuine flavour and taste of India, and other exotic locales. Whether we are privy to the private conversations of three young women plotting a desperate act in Bombay, imagining the details and scents of a British/tropical teahouse, or feeling a young wife's longing for the excitement of rioters in the streets, we meet true-to-life characters imbued with interest and complexity. These are rich stories, well-imagined, deeply felt." – Mark Frutkin, author, *Fabrizio's Return*, winner of the 2006 Trillium Book Award.

★ ★ ★

Twelve stories that provide startling glimpses of contemporary life in Bombay, and elsewhere. An innocuous jazz concert that awakens painful memories for a middle-aged professor and caregiver, a wealthy business woman compelled by the desire to hurt her best friend, an errant page that leads a journalist on a wild goose chase. Tales about friendship and repulsion, family ties and freedom; violence, public and private; ambition and uncertainty, alienation and acceptance, growing up and growing old.

★ ★ ★

Contact Veena and learn more at www.veenago.com/story